The House
of
Help

Rosemary Brierley

THE HOUSE OF HELP

The House of Help
by Rosemary Brierley

© Rosemary Brierley 2020

ISBN: 978 1 6579 5239 3

Cover Design
by Katrina Merkelt

www.rosemarybrierley.weebly.co.uk

THE HOUSE OF HELP

ACKNOWLEDGEMENTS

Special thanks to Frances Thimann
for her help and encouragement throughout
the writing and publication of this book.
Thanks also, to other members of
The Park Inn Writing Group, including
Anne McDonnell, Marion Bell and Di Peasey
for reading and critiquing
my early attempts at writing this novel.

PART 1

Gwyneth

Valerie

Paula

Susan

Nina

Christine

THE HOUSE OF HELP

CHAPTER 1

"You've got your troubles, I've got mine"
The Fortunes 1966

The letter said it wasn't far from the bus stop – turn left, up the steep hill. The once-grand Victorian mansions housing wealthy, upper-class families were now divided and crumbling homes for the single and unemployed. Some of these over-sized houses had signs of the changing times: *Bed-sit to Let* boards, rubbish overflowing from dustbins, CND posters in windows. But the one she was looking for had nothing to indicate who lived there, just the original number thirteen in the stained glass above the front door.

She rested her suitcase on the pavement, straightened up and rubbed the small of her back with both hands. The house had three storeys; at a window under the eaves, a girl rocked back and forth and appeared not to notice a visitor walking in through the gates. The drive swept in an arc to the front of the house then back to a second identical set of gates, forming a semi-circle around a well-tended rose-bed alongside the low wall which bordered the pavement.

Her feet scrunched over the gravel to the bottom of the stone steps where she hesitated, tempted to continue walking out of the other set of gates, and back down Granby Hill. But if she did, then where would she go? Not back to where she'd just come from; not back home to Wales. Not until it was all over. There was no alternative but to haul her case up to this house full of unfamiliar people and live with them as best she could for the next three months.

At the side of the door a long metal rod hung from the

3

wall. Was she meant to pull it? There was no need. One half of the double front door was opened at once by a young girl, her mousey-brown hair held back in a pony-tail. She looked at the newcomer's stomach before she looked at her face and said, 'You must be Gwyneth. Miss M told us you were coming.'

The girl wore a smock over a straight skirt, creating the impression of a partially opened umbrella. 'I'm Valerie,' she said as she beckoned Gwyneth inside.

The parquet floor and the wood-panelled walls were polished to perfection, but the oriental rugs were threadbare. The aroma of freshly-baked scones drifted up the corridor to one side the grand staircase.

Miss M's office was through the first door on the left of the hall. It was long and thin with a ceiling cornice on three sides: a section partitioned off from what had once been a much larger room. On the mantelpiece were two photographs: one a sepia print of a young woman with a feather in her hat, standing beside a military man, the other a boy of about six in short trousers and a sleeveless, Fair Isle pullover.

A woman with permed hair, the original blonde succumbing to grey, rose from one of two armchairs and said, 'Thank you, Valerie.' She waited as the girl with the pony-tail backed out of the room and closed the door. 'I'm Miss M. Do sit down, Gwyneth.' She removed a blanket crocheted in a rainbow of colours from the other armchair next to the spluttering gas fire. 'You can tell me about yourself.'

Gwyneth shrugged. 'What is there to tell?'

'Do your parents know?' Miss M sat down and leaned forward, her hands resting on the skirt of her Crimplene two-piece.

'Only Mam, no one else. They think I am in London looking after my auntie, see.' Lying was wrong. Chapel every week: Sunday school, then morning and evening services when she was seven, had convinced Gwyneth of that. But two months ago, when she left home, because she was beginning to "show", Mam had said it wasn't lying, not really. She was going to stay with Auntie Mair. But she's not ill, Gwyneth had protested.

'Sorry we couldn't take you before, but that's the rule, you see, six weeks before, six weeks after … The baby's father. Does he know?'

Gwyneth shook her head and swallowed hard. She avoided Miss M's eyes and stared instead at the dimple in the middle of the old lady's chin.

Miss M leaned down to take a tissue from the box on the hearth and passed it over. 'He has a right to know.'

'Mam says we can't tell anyone. It isn't right. It's against God.'

'You mustn't think like that. Every baby is a blessing. The girls who come here didn't plan to have them and some don't want them, but it was just a mistake, not a sin.'

Gwyneth shook her head and twisted the tissue around her fingers.

'Is he married, dear?'

Avoiding eye contact, Gwyneth focused on the antique desk in the corner of the room. The roll top was open to accommodate an untidy pile of papers. Behind it on the window sill stood a bottle of vodka not quite concealed behind the velour curtains.

'Much worse than that, it is.' Gwyneth started to shred the tissue into bits in her lap. 'He's …' Her explanation was interrupted by a tap on the door.

'Come in,' called Miss M.

Valerie stood in the doorway. 'Miss M, it's Paula. I think she's started.'

Miss M pushed herself up from her chair, lifted the spectacles that hung from a cord round her neck and put them in place before peering at a list drawing-pinned to the wall. 'Paula. She's not due for another ten days. Have you told Nurse Harding?'

'She's not here. Gone to the clinic to pick up the baby milk.'

'I'm coming. Paula probably needs a bit of reassurance that it's just her muscles on a practice run.' As Miss M walked towards the door she turned to Gwyneth. 'You'll be sharing a room with Valerie. She'll show you round.'

Gwyneth didn't want to be shown round; she wanted to go straight to her room and shut the door. She wanted to be on her own, but she couldn't be, could she? Not if she was sharing with Valerie who was now leading the way up the staircase. It was wide enough for two people to walk up side by side; the gleaming banister, supported by swirls of wrought-iron, curved round at the bottom. They passed a girl kneeling on the steps, polishing the brass stair-rods which held the threadbare carpet in place. The miniskirt she wore was not the most suitable outfit for the task. She turned her head as they passed and peeped around the straight fair hair which reached right down her back.

'Not finished, Susan?' asked Valerie.

Susan shook her head. 'I told Miss M. We mums shouldn't have to do chores, not when we've got bottles to make and nappies to wash.'

'What she say?'

'Married mothers who have a house to look after do their own housework. Not everyone has maids you know …' Susan pulled a face '… and anyway it will help to get your figure back in shape. Bloody cheek.'

'Should we look in on Chloe?' asked Valerie.

'Put your head round the door and listen, but don't wake her for Christ's sake.'

When they reached the first floor Gwyneth had no option but to leave her case and follow Valerie up a second narrower set of uncarpeted stairs to check on Susan's baby. At the top - the servant's sleeping quarters years ago when this house was built - four doors led off a small landing.

'Mums get a room on their own,' whispered Valerie. Then putting her fingers to her lips, she pushed open the door to a bedroom only just big enough to hold a single divan and a chest of drawers. Under the sloping roof next to the bed was a cot, made of canvas tacked to a folding wooden frame. Valerie beckoned to Gwyneth and they took three silent steps across the room and stared down at the baby swaddled in a white shawl. Its eyes were closed, and a soft grunting noise came from the pursed lips. 'She's lovely. Isn't she?' whispered Valerie.

Gwyneth didn't answer. For the first time since she'd found out at the beginning of June, Gwyneth thought of the thing that was growing inside her as not just a nuisance, but a baby. Up until now it had been something to ignore, while she concentrated on her A levels. And she'd succeeded in both ignoring it and passing History, Geography and Welsh. After the exams were over, she had been more concerned about her results than anything else. Her grades were good, so she could plan for a future; the pregnancy was something she had to endure, something that would soon be over.

Until now she had banished to the back of her mind the fact that when it was over, she would be leaving a baby behind. Gwyneth breathed in and pressed her lips tightly together, hoping that Valerie couldn't see the tears welling up in her eyes.

Valerie closed the door holding onto the handle so the catch fell back into place without a sound and whispered. 'She's just three weeks old.'

Gwyneth followed Valerie down the stairs to the first floor, picked up her case and they continued around the landing which surrounded the stairwell and into a room at the front of the house. 'This is ours. Us girls who are expecting have to share; we're lucky there's only the two of us in here just now.'

Faded purple pansies and yellow ribbons decorated the walls – even at home Mam didn't have wallpaper as old-fashioned as that. On one side of the room the flowers and bows had been hidden by posters of The Monkees, The Beatles and The Beach Boys. Well, The Beatles were OK, everyone liked The Beatles, but The Monkees …

Set into the chimney breast was a cast-iron fireplace; petals from a dozen red roses, arranged in an enamel milk jug, were scattered over the hearth. Above, on the mantelpiece, stood an assortment of greetings cards.

'Your birthday is it?' asked Gwyneth.

Valerie smiled. 'I was sixteen last week. How old are you?'

'Eighteen.'

Along the opposite wall, three iron bedsteads stood in a row. Valerie's bed was made, the covers tucked in with hospital corners. A teddy bear and a knitted giraffe were laid side by side with their heads on the pillow. On the other two beds folded blankets and sheets lay on the bare mattress.

'Miss M says that another girl will be here in a couple of weeks. Her name's Christine.'

Valerie opened the wardrobe and pointed to five empty coat-hangers to one side, then pulled open two drawers in the dressing table. 'You unpack. I have to go and peel the spuds for tea.'

When she'd gone, Gwyneth sat on the bed and shook her head. Six weeks of sharing with Valerie. How would she stand it? She was so young, so stupid and even seemed to like being pregnant. The way she'd cooed over the baby, maybe she wanted to be a sixteen-year-old mother. As Gwyneth made her bed she wondered about Christine, the girl who would also share their room. Would she be equally young and empty-headed? Would she chatter all night with Valerie about babies and boyfriends? Let's hope this baby came early then she'd get a room of her own like Susan. Susan had seemed alright: more Gwyneth's age and she did like her hair – just like Marianne Faithfull's. Gwyneth wished hers could be long and blonde. Not that it ever would. Hers was mousy-brown. She wouldn't have dared try to bleach it, but she had grown it and tried to iron it straight. Then her father had said she looked like one of them flower people, so she'd cut it again into the short curly style she'd had since she was a child. She bent down, flicked open the catches, flung back the lid of her suitcase and began to unpack.

A bell, like the one they rang at school playtime, summoned the girls to high tea at five-thirty. When Gwyneth found the dining room all the other girls were already standing behind their chairs down each side of a long refectory table.

'New girls always sit here.' Miss M, in her place at the head of the table, placed her hand on the back of the chair to her left. 'When we have a newcomer, everyone moves round.'

'Chairs of the music,' said an olive-skinned girl with long dark hair.

Several of the girls laughed.

'You mean musical chairs, Nina,' Miss M said then turned back to Gwyneth. 'So, our Ladies in Waiting … ' Miss M smiled, but the girls rolled their eyes at the expression which was probably not even amusing the first time she'd said it '… are all on the left, our mums on the right. The mum next to me is the one whose time with us is coming to an end.' The girl in this position attempted a smile. She wore the same red and black striped sweater as the girl Gwyneth had seen rocking back and forth at the upstairs window. Hastily applied make-up couldn't disguise the red eyes and blotchy cheeks.

Miss M said grace then everyone sat down, except two of the girls who dished out the cheese and potato pie.

'Have you seen Paula, Nurse Harding? How is she?' Miss M addressed the woman at the far end of the table. She was a good deal younger, taller and thinner than Miss M and wore a blue nurse's uniform and white starched cap.

'Oh, she only had a few twinges and got a bit anxious. I think it quite likely she'll go to term. But I said it might be best if she stayed in bed for the rest of the day so I've taken her tea upstairs on a tray.' The nurse spoke with a strong accent. Gwyneth would learn later that it was Australian. Nurse Harding was travelling the world and had already been to Singapore, India and Egypt which explained why she had a suntan in late October. She was only working at

The House to earn some cash so she could move on and see Europe.

When everyone had finished their cheese and potato pie, Miss M nodded and they all passed their plates around to the girls on table duty. They piled them up and carried them off to the kitchen, then returned with a tray stacked with white sliced bread. The girls spread it with butter – margarine as Gwyneth discovered when she tried it – and then with jam, Marmite or sandwich spread. To complete the meal, everyone received an equal small slice of Victoria sponge cake. No one left the table until everyone had finished.

Gwyneth's name was already on the washing up rota. She stood, belly pressed against the stone sink, and tried to avoid splashing water over her dress. If it got wet, she'd have to wash it tonight so it would dry tomorrow while she wore the only other item of clothing that would still fit her. Both garments had been made by her mother with plenty of room for expansion: this one was Black Watch tartan gathered onto the yoke above the bust-line, the other a tent-like creation in green and yellow, geometrically patterned material. After her baby was born, Gwyneth planned to burn them both.

'You can wear jeans, then. How is that?' she asked Nina who was scraping leftovers into the bin.

'I do bigger.' Nina lifted up the man's shirt she was wearing. 'The zip. I take it out and put in the stretchy material.' She pointed to a V shaped insert straining across her bump. 'I can do for you, if you want.'

Gwyneth shook her head. 'There is kind of you, but only six weeks more, it is.'

'Six weeks is long time.'

'What do we do now?' Gwyneth put the last saucepan upside down on the wooden draining board. 'Can we go out?'

'Out … at night!' Susan raised her plucked eyebrows as she added another dried plate to the pile on the kitchen table. 'You must be joking! Where would we go?'

After the washing-up was finished, Gwyneth crept past the doorway to the sitting room, saw the other girls huddled in a clique at the far end, and scurried upstairs. But there was nowhere to hide. Valerie found her lying on the bed and said the others were asking where she was and why she hadn't joined them. Gwyneth said maybe tomorrow and asked how often they could have a bath.

Valerie said twice a week and led the way to the bathroom. She demonstrated the art of lighting the geyser: 'Press the red button and hold it in while you turn the black knob, then jump back. It'll singe your eyebrows if you're not quick enough.'

With the blow-out that occurred when the pilot-light lit the gas, Gwyneth could well believe it.

But even here in the bathroom she couldn't hide. There was no lock on the door, just a piece of cardboard suspended by string around the handle – one side said *Engaged* the other *Vacant*.

The bath was a curved enamel tub supported on four claw-shaped feet. Gwyneth lay back and tried to avoid looking at the mound of her stomach which rose above the surface of the water like the back of a whale. She stared instead at the yellowish-brown stains on the enamel from the taps down to the plughole. She raised her eyes to the wall above and contemplated the copper geyser, the fire-raising dragon, now silent and exhausted after its tumultuous effort to produce six inches of lukewarm water.

At ten o clock precisely, Gwyneth heard the girls chattering as they climbed the stairs. She jumped out of bed and flicked off the light-switch, but didn't make it back under the covers before Valerie opened the door.

'What you doing in the dark?' Valerie switched on the light and picked up the book that Gwyneth had dropped in her haste. 'What you reading?

Gwyneth sighed. "Sons and Lovers."

'D.H. Lawrence?' Valerie smirked. 'One of the girls at school had a copy of Lady Chatterley.'

Gwyneth decided to change the subject. 'Going to keep your baby, are you?'

'They say we can't. We're too young … but Brian and I aren't going to let them take her away.'

'Her? How do you know it's a girl?'

'We always say her because Brian wants a girl. Me, I don't mind.'

'Known Brian long, have you?'

'Oh ages. Were at school together. Started going out in the third form.'

Somewhere above them a baby began to wail. Valerie began stuffing her pillows under the covers. 'Here, give me one of yours. I'll need it as well.'

'What for?'

'If Miss M comes around, it'll look as if I'm in bed.' Valerie stopped and stared at Gwyneth. 'You won't tell on me, will you?'

'Where you going, then?'

'Said if Chloe wouldn't settle, I'd go up and help.'

'Susan's baby. How do you know it is her?'

Valerie looked up. 'Her room's up there.' She pointed to

the ceiling then to the empty fireplace. 'Noise comes down the chimney.' Putting her finger to her lips, she opened the door and tiptoed out onto the landing.

Moonlight illuminated the unconvincing bump under the bedcovers; the baby's cries continued; footsteps above paced back and forth. Gwyneth stared up at the bare light bulb that dangled at the end of a flex suspended from an ornate rose in the centre of the ceiling. From this circle of moulded plaster, a damp and flaking patch seeped outward.

The wailing from above stopped. When Valerie returned, Gwyneth was still contemplating whether the dark stain in the ceiling resembled the coastline of Anglesey, the island where she'd spent her childhood but so hastily left.

'Fast asleep now. Rubbed baby's back and she gave this enormous burp.' Valerie tossed the pillow she'd borrowed back to Gwyneth and got into bed. 'It's the bottle, you know. If you breast feed, they don't get so windy.'

'How is it you know so much about babies, then?'

'Brian's got four younger brothers. Used to go round. Help him baby-sit. That's when …' Valerie looked down at her bump. '… it happened. Only did it once. Most nights we never managed to get them all to bed, before his mum and dad got back.'

CHAPTER 2

"What Becomes of the Broken-hearted"
Jimmy Ruffin 1966

Gwyneth looked around at the other eighteen girls at the breakfast table and tried to remember their names. There was Valerie, of course, Susan, the Marianne Faithfull look-alike, whose baby, Chloe, had kept them awake most of last night. Then at the far end next to Nurse Harding was the olive-skinned girl with the foreign accent. What was her name? Nina, that was it. The one sitting in the chair that had been empty the night before, her dark hair cut short into the nape of her neck, shaped round her ears then back-combed into a beehive like Helen Shapiro, must be Paula. For the rest she was still struggling to put names to faces.

'You not go to hospital yesterday, Paula?' asked Nina.

'Wish I had,' said Paula. 'Would be all over now, know whar I mean?'

'No, it wouldn't,' said one of the mums. 'It can take hours. You'd still be lying there in agony.'

The rest of the girls on the right side of the table joined in exchanging tales of long and painful labours, forceps and stitches, until Nurse Harding intervened and said they were scaring the girls who hadn't yet had their babies.

When breakfast was over, Miss M led the girls down the hall and into her office. She paused to pin on her hat, a turquoise pillbox covered with ruched satin. Then she opened a door at the far end and the girls followed her into a room lit solely by candles. As Gwyneth's eyes adjusted to the darkness, she could make out a gilt crucifix on the far wall and two candlesticks on a table covered with a purple silk cloth. Before it, arranged in rows, were polished chairs with hard seats. Attached to each straight back were wooden boxes, just big enough to hold a Bible and a hymn book for the use of the person seated behind.

Miss M took her place at the front and the girls filed in and remained standing. Maybe Gwyneth had sung the first hymn before but she couldn't be sure because back home the words were always in Welsh. Here there was no organ and it was up to Miss M to keep time and tune. Half the girls opened and shut their mouths but no sound emerged. The others made an effort including Nina, who did her best to pronounce some of the unfamiliar words, loud enough to be heard above everyone else. Then the girls - even those whose baby was imminent - had to kneel on hand-embroidered hassocks while Miss M recited a prayer. They remained on their knees for a further two minutes of silent prayer then struggled to their feet for the final hymn.

As Gwyneth followed the other girls out through Miss M's office into the hall, she couldn't help comparing the small, windowless room they'd just left with Moriah, the chapel that until a few months ago she'd attended every Sunday. It had tall stained-glass windows, a pulpit from which the minister looked down on his congregation and an altar-rail where they knelt for communion. Here the chapel was no bigger than the parlour back home and the altar a trestle table covered with a cloth.

'Miss M's quite something,' Paula whispered. 'D'yer know I've been here three weeks now, that's twenty-one church services, and she's never said the same prayer twice.'

Gwyneth frowned. 'Church every day, is it?'

'For our sins,' said Susan. 'To make us repent.'

'An ask God's forgiveness.' Paula sniffed.

'That man Miss M was talking about in the prayers. Who is he?'

'You mean Mr Percival Arlington-Smythe, our generous benefactor.' Susan smiled. 'He owned this house. Left it to the church so long as they made it into a home for girls in trouble.'

'Why did he do that, then?'

'Had no children to leave it to, not legitimate ones anyway - though they do say he had several that weren't.' Susan raised her neatly plucked eyebrows.

'Never!'

'His wife was the one with the money. After she died, he tried to find them – his children – but they didn't want to know. Said it was their mothers that needed his help all them years ago. So, to ease his conscience he left this place to girls like us.'

Miss M popped her head out of the office door and called out, 'Girls, come on now, it's time you were about your duties … and Gwyneth, the letter from the clinic, your coupons and allowance book. I forgot to ask for them yesterday. Nip up and get them for me now. Will you, dear?'

As Miss M's door closed, Gwyneth looked at the other two. 'Allowance book. What is that, then? Coupons?'

'Yer know, coupons for the milkman, the book you take to the post office every week,' said Paula.

'But I don't have them.'

'Don't worry. I didn't,' said Susan. 'Still don't, actually. Miss M wanted me to go down to Social Security, but I said there's no way I'm going down there to sit in that waiting room with all those scummy people.'

Paula pulled a face. 'It's alright for you. You don't know

nothin'. Your Daddy sends Miss M money for your keep. Some of us aren't so lucky.'

Gwyneth left Susan and Paula bickering, went up to her room and pulled her suitcase out from under the bed. In the pocket inside was the letter from the Clinic. She'd be glad to be rid of it, but she still wouldn't be able to blank out the memory: walking into the waiting room all eyes upon her, slouching down on the chair with her eyes closed trying to make herself invisible. Then a voice thick with disapproval called out her name and she was led into a room where white tiles glared from every wall. She lay on the black-vinyl mattress, the blood rushing to her head when they told her to raise her legs and they clamped her heels into metal claws. She'd stared at the circular light hanging from the ceiling and endured the indignity. Then the nurse was pulling off her rubber gloves, one finger at a time. Two weeks later she'd had to force herself to go back to the Clinic to collect the results because without them she wouldn't be admitted to *The House of Help*.

In the office she handed the letter to Miss M. Gwyneth hadn't even been tempted to steam it open because she knew she couldn't possibly have VD. She'd only been with one man and he'd never been with another woman, she was quite sure of that. What had happened between them had been something special, exciting, to seal their love for each other. What had happened since: the things her mother had said, the things they had done at the Clinic now made it dirty and sinful.

Miss M open the envelope and scanned the single sheet of paper inside. 'That's fine dear.' She threw the letter in the bin. 'I'm sorry you had to go through all that, but I'm afraid it's the rules … Now have you got your allowance and milk-token books?'

Gwyneth shook her head.

'Then you must go down to Social Security and put in a claim. You can go with Valerie. Now she's sixteen she's also entitled to apply for Supplementary Allowance.'

***

They sat side by side on the hard, plastic chairs in the Social Security office. Valerie had number 71; Gwyneth number 72. The last number called had been 33. Next to them sat a young woman whose runny-nosed toddler squirmed about on her knee and screamed that he wanted to get down. She didn't appear to hear the child's protests and continued talking to the woman next to her, who at intervals shouted, 'Give Over' to her young son who was chasing another dirty-faced little boy up and down between the rows of seats. Why on earth, thought Gwyneth, would anybody want children?

Although she had brought her book, she had no chance to read it: Valerie talked non-stop. By the time their turn came, Gwyneth knew how many baby-grows, vests, nappies and muslin squares she had in her layette and which of Brian's relatives had knitted the matinee coats, the bootees and the bonnets.

'Number 71.'

As Valerie got up and walked over to the counter, Gwyneth couldn't help wondering what would happen to all these tiny clothes wrapped in tissue paper if the baby was adopted. How would Valerie cope if, in the end, they took her baby away?

'Number 72'

The man behind the glass screen looked up as she sat down. Partitions divided the counter into supposedly private booths. However, over to her left Gwyneth could hear Valerie telling the clerk that she wouldn't need the money for long, because as soon as her boyfriend got a job, they'd be married. Cigarette smoke drifted in from the right.

'Name?'

'Gwyneth Hughes.'

'Is that Mrs?'

'No, Miss.' Miss M had warned her that if she said Mrs, they'd tell her to go home and send her husband to make the claim.

'Address?'

''13 Granby Hill.'

A smirk passed over the young clerk's face. 'Shall I put that down as a temporary?'

'Yes.'

'And your permanent address?'

'Don't have one,' said Gwyneth.

'National Insurance Number?'

'I don't know, I'm still at s… I have never worked.' She watched as he put a line through the rest of the questions.

He swivelled the form round to face her, pushed it under the glass partition and said, 'Sign here,' pointing to a space at the bottom.

'So, what do we do when we get back, then?' Gwyneth asked on the walk home.

'Chores,' said Valerie. 'Mums only have to fit in a bit of polishing or dusting while the baby's asleep, but Miss M says us Ladies in Waiting have too much time on our hands. You and I are on cleaning this week, then we change over to kitchen duty on Monday.'

When they arrived back, Valerie headed straight for the kitchen. 'I thought so,' she said, peering at a handwritten list pinned to the notice-board. 'All the cushy jobs are gone.' She indicated ticks and initials against Sitting Room, Dining Room, Chapel, Miss M's office, Nursery, Medical Room and Sickbay. 'It's only the bathrooms left. After lunch you take first floor front. I'll do the back.'

It was two o'clock when Gwyneth began squirting Harpic down the lavatory pan. Next, she tackled the bath; her back ached as she leant over the side and scrubbed at the greasy tide-mark. It wasn't fair expecting her to do this at 34 weeks pregnant.

At half past three Valerie came to find her.

She leaned on the door frame and watched as Gwyneth cleaned the soot off the tiles behind the geyser. 'You don't need to do that, you know, just a quick wipe round and most people are finished in half an hour.'

'My Dad says cleanliness is next to Godliness.'

'My Dad says there's no God and anyone who believes in all that rubbish needs their head examined.'

***

After tea Gwyneth put the last of the cutlery away in the drawer and tried to slip out of the kitchen unnoticed.

'Not creeping upstairs to hide again are you?' said Susan.

'Well I thought …'

'Come and join us. We won't bite.'

She'd not ventured into the sitting room before. It was of ballroom proportions. Just inside, on either side of the door, were two settees. Valerie was sitting on one of them, holding hands with a lad not much older than herself.

As Gwyneth passed by, she called out, 'This is Brian.'

The boy mumbled something but didn't look up.

'We're allowed visitors until half past eight but can't take them upstairs.'

'Don't know why.' Susan laughed. 'Can't get into much more trouble, can we?'

Most of the girls were seated at the far end of the room, around the marble fireplace, the grate now replaced with a hissing gas fire with cracked mantles.

Susan pointed to one of the dozen or so assorted armchairs. 'Sit there next to Paula. It used to be Maggie's place but she left last week.'

Paula flipped open the top of a packet of Embassy and offered Gwyneth a cigarette.

'Oh … No, I don't smoke.'

'Anyone else want a ciggie?'

The girl sitting on Gwyneth's other side took one then struck a match and leant across to give Paula a light.

Gwyneth tried hard not to cough.

On the television, a hair-netted Ena Sharples was drinking a milk stout in the snug of the *Rover's Return*, but only half the girls were watching. The others were knitting tiny garments in white or pale-yellow wool. In the bay-window was an ironing board with a basket of crumpled clothes to one side, piles of neatly-folded garments to the other. Presiding over it all was Nina.

One of the girls called out, 'Why don't you leave that, Nina. Come and sit down. You've only a few days to go.'

'No. I like to iron. When I iron, I not think.'

'You mean about Richard.'

'Pah! Richard! It is not good to think about him.'

***

'Richard, is he the father of Nina's baby?' Gwyneth asked later that night, after lights out.

'Yes,' Valerie replied from the other single bed under the window. 'He's married to the woman who hired her as an au-pair.'

'Shame on him!'

'But Nina doesn't talk about it.'

There were others, however, who had to tell everyone about the guy who had got them into trouble. Maybe it was their way of convincing themselves that, unlike what the outside world believed, they weren't solely to blame.

'If only I hadn't gone to the dance,' said Susan in the sitting room the following evening. 'But I couldn't not go, could I? We'd heard that the Raves up at the American base were fab; all the other girls were going. We were dancing when my friend nudged me and told me not to look but there was a GI who couldn't take his eyes off me. And sure enough he came over. Really good looking – hair combed back in a quiff the spitting image of Elvis. And he could dance – Jive, Twist anything. I just followed his lead and everyone stopped to stare and clapped when we'd finished. He bought me Rum and Coke.'

'Port and Lemon,' interrupted Paula. 'That were my downfall.'

'Didn't have that many,' continued Susan. It seemed so romantic. During the slow numbers, he held me close and didn't try anything. I could see the other girls watching, wishing they were me. After the last dance I couldn't bear to leave him, so when he offered to drive me home in his jeep I said yes. But once we were on our own, he was different, wouldn't take No for an answer.'

'So, what did he say when he found out that you'd fallen for a baby?' asked Gwyneth.

'I tried to tell him but whenever I phoned, his mates said he wasn't there.' Susan wound a tendril of hair round her index finger. 'So, my Dad went to see the commanding officer, who said he couldn't be responsible for what his men did in their own time and told him that Brad had a wife back in Pittsburgh. But he's not getting away with it. He's going to pay for what he's done. Dad's got his solicitor on the case. We're asking a few thousand at least in compensation.'

'But you not need the money.' Nina rested the iron on its heel. 'You not keep the baby.'

***

Miss M said that Gwyneth must go to Florrie's to book a bed for the birth, and explained that she'd have no trouble finding it. It was on the High Road and there was a stork in the front garden.

And indeed, there was! In the narrow strip of bare earth between the railings and the ex-Victorian workhouse, a sculpted bird, which had once been white, teetered on two spindly metal legs; half of its bill was missing and Gwyneth wondered if once it had dangled a baby in a sling. Next to it stood a wooden sign, *Florence Fancourt Maternity Home* in faded gold lettering. Another sign, the word *Wards* and an arrow in white on a blue background, pointed inside the old building. A similar blue and white sign directed outpatients round the side to a single-storey prefab with an assortment of pushchairs and prams parked outside.

As Gwyneth pushed open the door, she released the noise: children crying and shouting, and the smell: Jeyes fluid mingled with the odours it was trying to eliminate.

'Ante-natal card.' A woman seated at a desk just inside the door held out her hand. When Gwyneth looked blank, she said 'Don't you have one. Why not?'

'Just moved here, I have.'

The woman hesitated then lowered her voice. 'You're

not from *The House* are you?'

Gwyneth nodded.

'Give me your name and sit over there.' She indicated where women in various stages of pregnancy sat on a row of plastic chairs. 'When I'm ready, I'll call you over.'

'Your first?' asked the woman on the next seat, her belly pushed forward, her legs splayed out. Without waiting for an answer, she continued, 'My fourth. The first's over there.' She pointed to a boy of about three balancing on the windowsill. The second was a girl of about two, ripping pages out of a magazine, the third, a bald-headed baby sucking a dummy, sat on the floor at her feet. She patted her stomach and grinned. 'Couldn't believe it when I found I'd fallen for this one.'

How could people be so stupid, thought Gwyneth. Didn't this woman know about the pill?

'Mrs Hughes.'

'Mrs Hughes.'

The mother of three, soon to be four, gave Gwyneth a nudge. 'That you?'

'Oh … Oh. Yes.'

She walked over and sat down at the receptionist's desk. 'It's not Mrs.'

'All ladies here are Mrs…' The woman filled in the address on the card. '… especially those living at *The House*, or I'll have your Miss M coming down here again and telling me that you girls are to be treated just the same and given the same respect as other mothers … Not that I agree with her, mind.' She handed over the card. 'Here, doctor'll fill in the rest.'

The doctor was female. She checked Gwyneth's blood pressure, tested the sample she'd brought with her in a jamjar, prodded her tummy.

'Right. Everything's fine. We'll see you again in four weeks. You'll see your midwife in the meantime. Who is your midwife by the way?'

Gwyneth shrugged.

The doctor looked down at the card. 'Ah, *The House*. Well it'll be Nurse Watkins … no, no she's left. Can't keep up. The nurses up there keep changing so often. But I guess Miss M's still there. Lovely lady Miss M.'

Another five weeks of this, thought Gwyneth on the bus heading back to *The House*. Well, it could be worse, she supposed. At least now she'd got away from Uncle George. Why didn't Auntie Mair do the same? She wasn't sick. Well not like what people usually meant when they said sick. She was sick in the head. She must be to stay with that creepy husband. Always crying she was and saying he couldn't help it when he blasphemed or hit her. Why didn't she do something about it? I should have told her, thought Gwyneth, told her why I always went out, never stayed there when Uncle George was in, wedged the chair under the handle of the door every night. I should have told her what her husband had tried to do – and me seven months gone – told her he'd said that I'd already shown what kind of girl I was, so why wouldn't I do it with him too. Gwyneth drew stick people in the condensation on the inside of the bus window, then rubbed them out with her sleeve. Well at least she didn't have to see Auntie Mair or Uncle George ever again.

***

It was a few days later that Nina was taken to Florrie's. Her labour had started in the early hours and only Valerie, pacing the floor with Susan's baby, had seen the blue flashing lights of the ambulance. The others learnt from Miss M at breakfast next morning that Nina had given birth to a nine-pound baby boy.

Everyone missed Nina while she stayed in hospital for the compulsory ten days after the birth. The morning hymn singing wasn't the same: more subdued, less enthusiastic, more like a dirge without Nina. The other girls now had to choose between wearing crumpled clothes or doing their own ironing.

'When's Nina getting back?' Susan frowned at the knitting pattern in her hand.

Paula half turned so she could still see what was happening on Coronation Street. 'Not until Thursday.'

'She was going to show me how to make buttonholes.' Susan threw the almost-finished pink matinee coat onto the floor. 'Now it will never be finished in time.'

'When is it you leave, then?' asked Gwyneth.

'Tomorrow afternoon. Miss M takes Chloe to the adoption agency in the morning. I wanted her to be dressed in something I'd made. Did want to give her a locket with my picture inside, for when she's older, but they said that wasn't allowed. I've got a lock of her hair and the bootees she wore, but now she'll have nothing of mine.'

'Send the knitting with her' said one of the other girls. 'Perhaps her new mum will finish it.'

'No, she can't! She can't do that.' Susan rushed out of the room.

The door slammed shut and the girls stared at each other in silence.

Then Gwyneth bent down, picked up the knitting and stared at the narrow strip just a few inches long.

'It's the front facing,' said Paula and reached over for the pattern. 'Now let's see.' She scanned the middle pages then turned to the back. 'Right, it says work two inches in rib, she's done that. Now rib four, cast off four … give it 'ere. I'll do it.'

Later Gwyneth's offer to sew the front facing in place was accepted, but by ten o'clock the tiny pink garment still wasn't finished, so Paula took it upstairs and sewed on the pearl buttons by torchlight.

The following morning, the completed matinee coat was next to Susan's cereal bowl on the breakfast table. There were tears in her eyes as she brushed her fingers over the soft wool. Unable to speak, Susan just gave a weak smile and a nod of thanks, when Miss M said that it was all down to Paula and Gwyneth.

***

It was Tuesday, the day the vicar took morning prayers. He stood behind the lectern as usual eyeing up the girls as they filed into the chapel. His wrinkled hands were clasped together in front of his cassock, his fingers interlinked, his thumbs rotating around each other. The hymn singing was better now that the vicar knew the tune and the rest were able to follow his lead. As they sang *Guide me O Thou great Redeemer*, Gwyneth stared at the fleshy neck overhanging his dog-collar, the white sideboards joined together by a pelmet of hair which extended around the back of his head beneath a bald pate dotted with brown pigment spots.

During the sermon the vicar stared at Susan and said, 'Those of you whose time here is coming to an end must remember the lessons learned in the last year. You must ask God's forgiveness for past sins, for his guidance in keeping to the straight and narrow path of righteousness when you return and take up your place in the outside world and for his strength to resist the temptations of the flesh.'

'Bollocks,' muttered Susan.

Gwyneth wondered if the vicar had heard her but doubted it when she noticed behind his earlobe the pink plastic crescent with the tube leading inside his ear. But then, as they all filed out, he asked Susan to stay behind.

'No, he didn't hear me swear,' said Susan when she came to join the others almost a quarter of an hour later. 'Actually, he just went on and on about where did I live, did I go to church, how he could tell me where my nearest church was, could write to the local vicar and all the time he had his beady eye on my tits and kept trying to look up my skirt.'

'Well, your skirt is very short,' said Valerie.

Susan went up to her room to feed Chloe. When she didn't come down for morning coffee, Paula, Gwyneth, Valerie and Nina went upstairs to make sure she was alright. In the tiny attic room Susan was sitting on the bed, not moving, staring at the baby lying in the canvas cot under the eaves. The tiny clenched fists boxed the air while the blue eyes stared up at the flaking plaster. She was wearing the pink matinee coat.

'It suits her, don't you think?' said Susan.

'She looks so cute,' said Valerie.

'Lovely,' said Paula.

Gwyneth didn't know what to say but felt the beginnings of a tear forming beneath her eyelid.

'You have camera?' asked Nina. 'I can take photo of Susan and baby and then you all together.'

'You'll need a flash,' said Paula.

Susan rummaged through her half-packed suitcase. 'Here.' She handed a camera and flash bulbs to Nina.

At half past eleven, Miss M was standing in the hall

wearing her turquoise hat and looking at her watch. Susan came slowly down the stairs carrying her baby. When she got to the bottom, she stopped and kissed Chloe's cheek and tickled her miniature palm so that the hand that peeped out from the pink knitted sleeve curled around her forefinger. Miss M held out her arms. Susan took one last look at the blue eyes staring back at her, the eyebrows raised, creasing the tiny forehead.

Miss M put her hand under the baby's head, then took the weight of the tiny body on her other arm as Susan let go. 'Now, chin up, dear. Remember your father will be here shortly and you'll be going home.'

Susan turned and fled back up the stairs.

She was still in her room when, at two o'clock precisely, a man with a moustache, wearing a pinstriped suit, arrived. Nurse Harding took him into the office to give his daughter time to say her goodbyes.

The girls stood in the doorway to wave Susan off. As her father held open the door of his Jaguar, Susan turned and said, to no one in particular, 'The vicar, he said I could still get married in white.'

CHAPTER 3

"Somewhere my Love"
(Lara's Theme from the film Doctor Zhivago)
The Ray Conniff Singers

There had never been any doubt in Gwyneth's mind; she was not keeping her baby. She hadn't planned to have it, and now she was carrying it, she still didn't want it. She could no more bring up a child on her own than she could walk across the Menai Straits. She wasn't like Nina who'd said all along that she would never be parted from her baby.

When they arrived back from the hospital, Nina and her baby were already bound together. Her son was held tight beneath Nina's breasts, suspended in a sling made from a long length of material wound around both bodies crossed over at the back and tied tightly in place round her waist. All that was visible was spiky, dark hair, and closed eyes. Occasionally long eyelashes fluttered open and blue eyes looked out from the folds of fabric with an air of contentment. The baby only came out when his nappy was changed. He stayed put for his feeds as Nina's nipples were there right next to his mouth – when he rooted around all she had to do was to unfasten a couple of buttons on her shirt and he would latch on. The arrangement was mutually convenient as the baby could suckle at will and Nina had her hands free to get on with the dusting and polishing, and the mountain of ironing that had accumulated during the ten days she'd been away.

'Babies must be put in their cots at meal time, Nina,' said Miss M when mother and baby came down to tea.

'But I cannot to leave him in my room.'

'There are cots in the nursery. You can put him in there. The other Mums do.'

'But he cries. He need all the time to be near to me.'

As if on cue, the sling against Nina's chest began to quiver, there was a high-pitched cry then a tiny fist pushed its way up through the folds of material.

'It's the rule. Can you imagine what it would be like if everyone brought their baby to the table? We'd have … what …' Miss M looked round the table counting. 'Eight babies to tea. It would be bedlam.'

Nina's baby was now crying continuously, only pausing now and then to take a breath.

'Babies shouldn't be spoilt,' said Nurse Harding. 'They need routine: feeding every four hours, not picking up whenever they cry.'

'Have you ever had a baby, Nurse Harding?' asked Paula.

'Of course not. I'm not married.'

Miss M broke the silence that followed. 'Well, I don't entirely hold with the strict routines of the past. Babies know when they're hungry and that isn't always every four hours, and they do need lots of cuddles, but I must agree with Nurse Harding that some of these modern ideas can lead to very spoilt babies and very tired mums.'

'In Greece it is different. The baby go everywhere with the mother: to milk the goats, to the fields to pick the olives.'

'I am sure you understand, Nina, that while you live here you must do as we do.'

Nina left the table. She came back alone and ate her sausage and mash without saying a word. From the nursery down the hall came a continuous whimper. After tea no one, not even Nurse Harding, dared to say anything when Nina dried the dishes with her baby back home in his sling.

Paula led the deputation to Miss M. Gwyneth would have joined them, but it would be hard enough to fit five pregnant girls and three mums in the office. So, she stayed in the sitting room talking to Nina.

'What will you call your baby?'

'In Greece we say baby until after we go to church for the name day.'

'When will you have that?'

Nina shrugged. 'I don't know.'

'Taking him back to Greece, are you?'

Nina paused in her ironing and looked down at the sleeping baby. 'No, there is no work in Cephalonia.'

'But your family, they are still there?'

'Only one brother. My mother and sisters, they die in the earthquake.'

'There was an earthquake!'

'I was seven. I remember the birds, they stop singing, the dogs they bark then the ground shake. 2,000 people die. Our house is gone. The people of Sweden they send houses in bits for us to fix together. But most of our goats are dead and the olive trees are gone. For twenty years my father grows those trees. He did not want to start again, so he die.'

'There is terrible. Who looked after you?'

'My brother. When he married, I go to Athens to stay with my aunt then get job to look after children. Then I come to England as au pair and I think everything is to be OK.'

'So now, where will you go?' asked Gwyneth.

'I find job, somewhere to live.'

'On your own with a baby, how will you manage?'

'I manage.' Nina shrugged. 'No one knows what is to

happen next week, next year.'

Paula appeared in the doorway and shouted across the room. 'It's OK, Nina. You can keep yer baby with you at the table.'

'Miss M, she say that?'

'Well, she said so long as the Ladies on the Committee don't find out.'

'The Ladies on the Committee. Who are they?' asked Gwyneth.

'The Church Committee that run this place, make the rules, tell Miss M what to do,' said Valerie from the settee next to the door where she sat holding hands with Brian.

'Why Miss M change her mind?' asked Nina.

'We all said we didn't mind and promised we wouldn't bring our babies to the table. But Miss M says that if any of yous …' Paula looked round at the other mothers. '… start whingein' about it, it'll have to stop.'

'It is OK,' said Nina. 'Me and my baby go soon. And thank you for to do this for me. When my baby was inside me, he hear my heart beat all the time. When he is here, he still can hear it.'

'Until now, I've never heard your baby cry. Not even at night,' said Valerie.

'At night he sleep beside me. I lie on my side and he can get his milk whenever he want.'

'Isn't that dangerous? Aren't you afraid that you'll roll over and squash him?'

'Oh no, that never happen.'

'Well,' said Paula. 'Whar ever you do, don't let Miss M or Nurse Harding find out. They'll go mental.'

***

At breakfast on weekdays Nurse Harding would read out a

list of the girls who were due for their ante-natal or post-natal checks. On Thursday 10 November, Gwyneth's name was among them as it was now two weeks since she'd been to the outpatient's department at Florrie's and two weeks before she was due to go back.

The medical room was near the front door on the opposite side of the hall to Miss M's office. Gwyneth hesitated before knocking. The first time she'd been to see Nurse Harding had been an unpleasant experience: it had been shortly after her arrival and she'd been given a long lecture about how she should have registered with an ante-natal clinic, how she should have been seen regularly by a doctor or midwife. Then all those questions – questions she wasn't prepared to answer.

She took a deep breath and knocked on the door.

'Come.'

Nurse Harding was washing her hands. Without turning around, she said, 'Gwyneth isn't it. Sit down.'

After drying her hands, Nurse Harding came over and sat behind the desk. She flipped through a pile of brown folders, pulled one out and opened it up.

'Ah yes, no ante-natal care before you came here.' Nurse Harding clicked her tongue. 'What if there's something wrong?'

There was something wrong, Gwyneth was sure of that, but going to the clinic wouldn't have made any difference, unless they'd offered her an abortion and they'd only do that if she told them … and she couldn't do that.

'And you won't say who the father is.' Nurse Harding stared at her across the desk.

If she told anyone, Gwyneth was certainly not going to tell this sour-faced woman in the starched apron.

'Perhaps you're not sure who the father is.'

'Of course I know. I haven't been going with anyone and everyone, if that's what you think.'

'Well no. It's just that we need to know if there's any health problems in his family that's all.'

'Only diabetes.'

'And what about your family?'

'Diabetes.' Gwyneth immediately regretted providing this potentially incriminating information and quickly added, 'Quite common around where we live it is.'

'Really,' said Nurse Harding, holding out her hand. 'Did you bring a urine sample?'

While the nurse tested her water, Gwyneth looked around the room. At the far end were two doors: she had been told that the one on the right led into Nurse Harding's bed-sitter, the one on the left into sickbay, a room hardly ever used except by girls in the early stages of labour, while they waited for the ambulance to take them to Florrie's.

'That's OK. No sign of sugar. Now, if you'd lie on the couch.'

In her hand Nurse Harding held a metal instrument the shape of a very large silver egg-cup. Gwyneth flinched as the rim of the cold metal cup touched her bare stomach. Nurse Harding put her ear to the other end and moved the "egg-cup" several times before exclaiming, 'There it is - the heartbeat.'

She continued the examination by prodding with her cold hands, concentrating on the area below Gwyneth's bump. 'That's good. The head's engaged.'

'Going to come soon, then, is it?'

'Impossible to tell. These babies they arrive when they're ready. You'll just have to be patient.'

***

Miss M decided that everyone needed cheering up: an outing perhaps. She'd put it to the Ladies on the Committee and they'd agreed to fund a trip to the cinema. *Doctor Zhivago* was deemed to be suitable. They would have to go in two groups on successive Saturday afternoons because of the babies. Mums would leave bottles already made-up and the girls who stayed behind would do the feeds. Miss M would take the first party while Nurse Harding held the fort. Then the following week they would swap over.

As it wasn't long until their babies were due, Gwyneth, Paula and Valerie were in the first party. Valerie asked if Brian could come too and Miss M said she didn't see why not, if Brian wanted to. Brian didn't. Nina of course would be bringing her baby, so everyone agreed it would be best if she was in Miss M's group.

They left *The House* on a cold November afternoon to walk down the hill and along the high street to the *Majestic*. Miss M was in the lead alongside Nina, who had found an old nurse's cape large enough to accommodate both herself and her son. Behind walked eight of the girls, six of them expecting. It was impossible not to notice how many people turned and stared.

'Hold your head high and ignore them,' said Miss M.

The young girl in the box office asked how many.

'Ten,' repeated Miss M.

'Eleven if you include Nina's baby,' whispered Valerie. 'Going in that is, but it might be more coming out!'

'Knock it off,' said Paula. 'I keep thinking: what'll I do if my waters break in there.'

'Well, it's very dark. I don't suppose anyone would notice.'

The usherette led the way, playing her torch on the steps in the aisle.

As they passed the double seats in the back rows, one of the girls said, 'Do you remember that other world we used to live in: Saturday night dates at the cinema?'

'An look where that gor us,' said Paula.

The girls followed the beam from the usherette's torch and squeezed their way between the rows, then flipped down a seat to sit on. Adverts flashed on the screen. Miss M passed a bag of pear drops down the line.

As the title sequences came up, the man sitting behind Miss M tapped her on the shoulder and asked her to remove her hat, which she did after a tussle with the pin holding it in place. The opening music grew louder; Nina's baby opened his eyes, rooted around, latched onto a nipple and began to suckle. Paula offered Valerie a cigarette, which she accepted after everyone had promised not to tell Brian. The two girls lit up and their smoke curled upwards to join the other swirls illuminated in the cone of light from the projector to the screen.

Gwyneth tried to hold back the tears as she watched the ill-fated couple say their goodbyes: Yuri off to search for his wife, Lara to join her daughter in the Urals. When the light went up for the interval Miss M was mopping her eyes with a lace handkerchief and some the girls were doing the same with their sleeves. The only member of the party unmoved by the scene was Nina's baby: satiated with milk he'd fallen asleep. An usherette was standing at the bottom of the central aisle near the screen, a tray suspended from a strap around her neck. The Ladies on the Committee had agreed that funds would stretch to an ice cream. The slimmer mums edged their way out along the row and back again with three cornets, three choc ices and four strawberry splits.

As the lights dimmed for the second half, Paula whispered to Valerie, 'I think I'm startin'.'

'Oh, not again, Paula,' said Miss M.

***

Paula's baby was due the following day, but she had no contractions – real or imaginary. In fact, nothing happened for a further week. Miss M said it was quite normal for first babies to be late, but Nurse Harding insisted that Paula must have got her dates wrong.

'Whar does she mean?' exclaimed Paula. 'Does she think I don't know when it happened. That I was having it away all the time. Bloody Cow!'

Paula had tried drinking orange juice and castor oil, but that didn't work, so Valerie and Gwyneth suggested a long walk. They walked down the hill to where the houses became smaller and were homes for just one family.

Valerie looked at the back to back terraces and said, 'Wouldn't it be nice to have a home of your own?'

'No,' said Gwyneth. 'That means a husband and I'm not wanting one of them yet.'

'Me and Gino never had a real home,' said Paula.

'If you lived together, why didn't you get married?' asked Valerie.

'He never asked.'

'So, why did you run off with him?'

'Why do you think? If me Dad had found out I was expecting he would have chucked me out anyway. He said, ever since I was little, "You ger into trouble then don't bother coming back." Me brothers would have beaten Gino up. So, I left home one morning, but didn't go to work.

Caught the bus to Blackpool instead.'

'Didn't your family wonder why you were taking a suitcase to work?'

'Well me three brothers are in the Merchant Navy so they weren't around. Dad was still in bed sleeping it off and our Mam goes out cleaning offices at six o'clock every morning.'

'Have you written to tell them you're OK?'

Paula shook her head. 'Never had time. It was high season so we got jobs in a hotel right away. Gino was a waiter, me a chambermaid. Told them we were married. They must have known we weren't from our cards, but didn't say anything 'cause we lived-in and could share the same room.'

'But I thought you said you lived in Fulham.'

'Gino decided it was best to leave Blackpool before the season was over. Get down to London before everyone came down looking for work. He got a job as a barman in Kings Road straight away. But me, I was showing by then and nobody wanted to take me on.'

'But you managed to get a flat alright?'

'I was wearing me coat when we went to look round. It was a month before the landlady realised I was pregnant and chucked us out.'

'Is that when Gino left?'

'Yea, said that he'd never wanted to be a dad in the first place. I should've been on the pill. And anyway, he couldn't stand these cold winters; he was going back to Italy.'

By now the three girls were climbing back up the hill, stopping at intervals to get their breath. As Paula stepped in through the front door of *The House* her waters broke. Gwyneth ran for a mop and bucket, Valerie yelled for Miss

M. Nurse Harding arrived and asked what all the fuss was about before helping Paula into sickbay.

As if making up for lost time, Paula's labour progressed at a pace: strong contractions were coming every few minutes and even the girls in their attic bedrooms heard Paula scream and call Gino a cheating, lying bastard and threaten to kill him.

Nurse Harding kept looking at her watch. 'I called the ambulance half an hour ago. Where are they?'

At the sound of footsteps on the front steps, Gwyneth flung open the front door. 'Oh, at last. Thank goodness you're here …'

On the top step stood a girl with acne and lank, greasy hair. 'Hello, I'm Christine.'

CHAPTER 4

"I just don't know what to do with myself"
Dionne Warwick 1966

First Paula, then, two days later, Valerie: the two girls that Gwyneth had got to know at *The House* both in hospital with their new babies and they wouldn't be home for at least another week.

Gwyneth went to Florrie's for her second ante-natal appointment. At least this time she knew what to expect and took a book to read while she waited. Not that she could concentrate amidst the wailing babies and tearaway toddlers.

Two hours wait to see a doctor to be told what she already knew: the head was engaged and the baby was due in ten days' time. He dismissed her with the words: 'If nothing happens in the meantime, we'll see you in two weeks.'

When Gwyneth had arrived, the sky had been clear; she emerged from the Outpatient Department to driving rain and deep puddles. Water gushed off the end of the stork's broken bill and streamed down its spindly legs. She sheltered a while in the porch of the main entrance and tried to decide whether to go for the bus and get very wet or stand there for half an hour or … she checked her watch. It was three fifteen. Visiting hour didn't end until four. She pushed open the heavy door, stepped into the narrow hallway and struck the brass bell with the palm of her hand. A lady popped her head out of a small hatch in the wall.

'Browne Ward?' said Gwyneth.

'First floor. Turn right.'

The ward was long, the walls covered with shiny, olive-green paint. Rows of bedsteads extended down each side under the tall sash windows. Valerie's bed was close to the door.

When she saw Gwyneth, she waved and called out, 'It's a boy. Did Miss M tell you? He looks just like Brian.'

Gwyneth looked down at the red, blotchy face and complete lack of hair and wondered where Valerie saw the resemblance.

'Brian saw him being born, you know.'

Gwyneth knew. It had been the talk of *The House*: how Valerie's son had been born in the ambulance. Apparently, she'd had contractions all day, but hadn't said anything because she was waiting for Brian. By the time he'd arrived and they'd told Nurse Harding, the head was already crowning. In the chaos that ensued no one noticed Brian sneak into the back of the ambulance.

'Brian was great, you know. Didn't faint or anything.' Valerie's eyes kept flicking back to the ward's double doors. 'Brian held my hand all the time. He wanted to hold the baby, but he couldn't because they hadn't cut the cord. But then, when we got to the hospital, they wouldn't let him in, because he wasn't my husband.' Valerie's tone suddenly changed from annoyance to elation. 'Then they wouldn't. But now, when it's visiting time, they can't stop him.'

If he hadn't come to a halt beside Valerie's bed, Gwyneth wouldn't have recognised Brian. Gone was the awkward youth in overalls, instead here was a grown-up in trousers pressed into a knife-edge crease, a clean white shirt and a tie. In his hand was a box of Cadbury's Milk Tray and on his face a huge grin.

'He's grand isn't he, my son. I always wanted a boy.'

Gwyneth was sure that Valerie had told her many, many times that it was a girl Brian wanted. No point in mentioning it now though. Instead she said, 'Paula is over by there. I'll leave you two together and go and see her.'

Paula didn't have any visitors. Her beehive hairdo had suffered and was now flat on one side and out of control on the other. The lack of make-up accentuated the dark circles under her eyes.

'There is a coincidence it is,' said Gwyneth. 'You and Valerie. Your babies both late, but when they come, they come so quick? I hope mine's like that.'

'You've gor no idea. I've never felt pain like it.'

Gwyneth raised her hand. 'Don't tell me. I don't want to know.'

She peeped into the cot at the end of the bed. The baby's skin was less blotchy and a shade darker than Valerie's baby and she had hair, a single jet-black quiff sticking up from the centre of her scalp. One of her hands had escaped from the swaddling blanket and she was sucking at her clenched fist.

'What is it you are going to call her?'

'Gina.'

'But that is nearly as bad as Valerie calling her baby Brian.'

Paula shrugged. 'Whar does it matter? Gino's not coming back.'

'He hasn't answered your letters, then?'

Paula shook her head. 'Let's talk about somethin' else. What's the new girl like?'

'You mean Christine?'

'Saw her as they took me out to the ambulance. Straight, mousey hair and spots. Why would any fellar want to do it with her?'

'She told me how it happened.'

'Immaculate conception?'

'This girl she knew wanted to visit her boyfriend in Birmingham, see, but her dad said she couldn't go on her own, so she asked Christine to go with her.'

'Why Christine?'

'None of her friends' parents would let them go, but Christine's Mum drinks, see. Doesn't know where she is half the time.'

'So, she went, but I still don't see.'

'The boyfriend's parents were away on holiday, so they spent the whole time in the bedroom.'

'So how come it's Christine that gets pregnant?'

'Le-Roy was there to make up the foursome, see. Best three days of her life it was, says Christine.'

'Le-Roy must have been gutted when she told him.'

'Doesn't know. Gone back to Jamaica her friend's boyfriend says.'

'Poor Christine,' said Paula.

Poor Christine. What about me thought Gwyneth. She longed to tell one of the girls her story. A couple of times she almost had, but something had stopped her. Perhaps it was her mother's words: It's unnatural. It's against God. Perhaps she was afraid of what the other girls would say. She doubted very much that they would say, poor Gwyneth.

When she came out of the hospital, Gwyneth was relieved to see it had stopped raining. As she walked to the bus stop, she thought of the bald-headed baby boy wearing the sleepsuit Valerie had shown her many times, the cuffs rolled up to reveal perfect hands, tiny fingernails. She thought of the baby girl with the dusky complexion, the wisp of dark hair peeping out from the shawl she'd watched

Paula knitting. Gwyneth hadn't bought anything for her baby; knitting hadn't crossed her mind. She still considered what was growing inside her to be a mistake, an inconvenience, not her fault and, definitely, not her responsibility.

Coming towards her was a man tapping the pavement with his white stick. Gwyneth stepped aside to let him pass, but didn't avert her eyes. Most of the other girls at *The House* would have panicked when they saw him, worried in case by looking at a blind man they'd give birth to a baby with a birthmark or a club foot. Gwyneth didn't believe these old wives' tales: she could have dealt with a mouse in the house or stepped on a black beetle without giving it a thought. If there was something wrong with her baby it had nothing at all to do with these silly superstitions. There was a much more logical explanation.

Incest it was, Mam said, and a baby that wasn't quite right would be God's punishment. Gwyneth greatest fear in all this was not for her unborn child but for herself. If the baby wasn't perfect then no couple would want to adopt it. She'd have to spend the rest of her life looking after it.

***

The ache low down in her back began one evening four days later. Gwyneth thought little about it: there were still five days to go and most of the other girls' babies had been late. She went to bed and slept reasonably well but woke at about five. She felt a faint tightening of her stomach muscles but then it was gone. Was this the beginning? She still wasn't sure. Gwyneth remembered how fed up Nurse Harding and the girls had been with Paula's false alarms and decided to try and go back to sleep.

By the time the "Getting Up" bell rang at seven she'd

had about another four of what she thought might be contractions. The one she felt during breakfast must have shown on her face, because Miss M asked if she was alright, but still Gwyneth didn't say anything. If Valerie or Paula had been there, she could have told them, but they were still in hospital. So, it wasn't until later that afternoon when she went to the toilet and discovered a reddish-yellow stain in her knickers that she decided to go to the medical room to see Nurse Harding.

'It's a show. Just a bit of blood-stained mucus. Shows your cervix is beginning to dilate,' Nurse Harding said as she held her hands upwards and pulled on a pair of rubber gloves.

Gwyneth lay on the examination couch, drew up her knees and let her legs fall apart. She stared up at the cracks in the ceiling and held her breath as Nurse Harding put her fingers inside her.

'It's only the early stages yet.' Nurse Harding straightened up and began pulling off the gloves, finger by finger. 'But I think we'll send you to Florrie's anyway. Then they can keep an eye on you.'

'Why, something wrong, then, is there?'

'No, no of course not. Is there anyone we should call to let them know you're in hospital?'

'No. No one.'

Once Gwyneth arrived at the hospital the contractions stopped. She was put in the ante-natal ward with other Mums-to-be who gossiped about their husbands. Gwyneth hid her ringless finger under the blanket and silently thanked Miss M for the title Mrs in front of her name on the card clipped to her bed. When asked if her husband would be coming in to see her Gwyneth shook her head and said he worked away. Did she imagine it, or did the other women exchange knowing glances?

But then it didn't matter what the other women thought. There were more pressing things to worry about. The nurse approached the bed carrying a metal dish, which she placed on the bedside locker while she drew the curtains around the bed. The bowl contained a razor and what looked like a small tube of toothpaste. She pulled back the bedcovers and motioned to Gwyneth to lift her nightdress.

'It's alright. There's no need to look so frightened, I'm only going to shave you.' The nurse scraped away at the thick black hair beneath Gwyneth's bump. 'It's to prevent infection. Now lift up your knees and open your legs.'

Gwyneth did as she was told and lay motionless, her eyes screwed shut to hold back the tears. Tears of embarrassment as she lay there submitting herself to the indignity of a stranger peering at her private parts and scraping away with a razor.

'There, all done. See, that wasn't so bad, after all. Was it? Now turn over and lie on your left side.'

'Why?'

'Nothing to worry about, just an enema,' the nurse said as she squeezed the contents of the tube into Gwyneth's bottom.

She shivered as the cold slime forced its way inside her and no longer could she keep back the tears.

'Hold onto it as long as you can, then there's the toilet over there.' The nurse pointed to the far end of the ward.

When her tormentor had gone, the woman in the next bed leaned across and whispered, 'I'd go now if I were you. Don't want someone to get in there before you.'

Gwyneth shuffled down the ward to the toilet, locked

herself inside and sobbed. When she returned to her bed the midwife was waiting to examine her again. She was very fat and smelt of smoke and Gwyneth didn't like her at all.

'It will be ages yet,' she said as she pulled off her rubber gloves.

'How long?'

The midwife shrugged. 'Might be before midnight. Might be after.'

Gwyneth looked at the clock. It was just after seven. She tried to read her book, *The Midwich Cuckoos*, but thinking how even the old spinsters of Midwich became pregnant through no fault of their own gave her no comfort. She read the same words over and over as she waited for the next contraction to come.

At ten o'clock the lights on the ward were dimmed and the nurses pulled the curtains around the beds. One by one the bedside lights were switched off and the women settled down to sleep. Now there was no sound at all on the ward and although there were a dozen or more women close by, they were strangers and Gwyneth had never felt so alone.

The midwife had placed a buzzer beside Gwyneth's hand and told her to press the button if the pain got too bad. But what was bad? It was bad already. Several times her finger hovered above the buzzer but then in her mind she saw the irritated expression on the face of the midwife called back from her cigarette break. She didn't press it.

Then just before midnight Gwyneth felt an overwhelming urge to bear down and push the baby out. She pressed the buzzer.

'Oh! Don't do that. Don't push yet,' said the midwife when she'd felt around with her fingers once again. 'Not yet. You're not fully dilated. Push now and you'll tear, you'll need stitches.'

Try as she might she could not stop herself from pushing and why would she want to stop anyway. She just wanted it all over. Then she thought of Susan. How Susan had complained of the pain "down below". How Susan had told them how she had got a hand mirror, put it between her legs, so she could see what they'd done, and counted more than a dozen black stitches. Gwyneth tried harder to stop herself from pushing.

At four o'clock in the morning, the midwife decided that the birth was imminent; Gwyneth was bundled into a wheelchair and trundled down the corridor to the delivery room. All four walls were covered from floor to ceiling with the same white tiles; in the centre stood a stainless-steel table, covered with a thin black mattress, under a large circular light suspended from the ceiling. Gwyneth put both feet on the floor so the wheelchair came to a halt in the doorway.

'Don't be silly. Pick your feet up or you'll hurt yourself,' said the midwife.

Fearing she may wake the others on the ward, up until now Gwyneth had only screamed inwardly when the pain reached its height. Here, when it reached a crescendo, she just let it all out and her screams bounced off the tiled walls.

'Now there's no need for all that noise, is there?' said the midwife.

'But why, why? Why is this happening to me? I don't want a baby.'

'You should have thought about that while you were having your "bit of fun" nine months ago,' said the midwife.

Gwyneth stared at her superior smile. What was she? Twenty-five, thirty maybe, no ring on her finger, probably never had a boyfriend? What did she know? What right had she to criticize? The pain came again and Gwyneth began to writhe around on the mattress.

'Here try this.' The midwife pressed a mask over Gwyneth's nose and mouth.

She struggled and tried to push it away, then Gwyneth caught a whiff of pear drops laced with rubber and remembered Paula telling her about gas and air. She lay back and inhaled the intoxicating fumes.

As the contraction died away the midwife's head popped up from between Gwyneth's legs and appeared over the mound of her stomach. 'The head is crowning. With the next contraction you must push.'

There was little space between contractions now.

'Push, push. You're nearly there.'

But she wasn't. It took another ten minutes and more contractions before the head emerged. Then Gwyneth felt the rest of the wet, slippery body slide out with no effort from her at all. It was over.

She heard the baby's cry and the words: 'It's a girl.'

'So, there was no need for all that silly fuss was there?' said the midwife. 'Now we must get rid of the afterbirth.' She began to press down on Gwyneth's stomach.

Gwyneth lay on the metal trolley in the delivery room covered by a single sheet. 'Won't be a minute,' the nurse had said. 'Just going to find someone to stitch you up.' But that must have been ages ago. Next to her in a cot lay her baby wrapped in a sheet, only its head visible. No port wine stain: in fact, its face appeared normal ... or was it? Gwyneth stared at the half-closed eyes. Were they slanting like the boy from the village, who didn't go to school? The one they called a mongol. And what about the rest of it. Did it have the right number of fingers, the right number of toes? Were its legs, its arms twisted or deformed?

She kept seeing her mother's face, hand clapped over her mouth, the horror in her eyes. 'No good ever came of close family having …' and her words had tailed off, never finishing her sentence. But to Gwyneth her meaning had been clear.

A nurse in a dark blue uniform put her head round the door. 'Everything alright in here? Oh! Are you all on your own? They shouldn't have left you.'

Startled by the sudden noise the baby began to cry. Sister came into the room, picked it up and made shushing noises as she swayed back and forth, but the baby continued to cry.

Gwyneth began to cry too.

'There, there, dear. What's the matter?'

'I want to go home, everything to be like it was …' Gwyneth looked over at the cot. ' … before this all happened.'

CHAPTER 5

"You don't have to say you love me"
Dusty Springfield 1966

The nurse lifted the baby out of the perspex crib and laid it on a sheet she'd already spread out on the bed. She looked at Gwyneth and inclined her head towards a young man in a white coat striding down the ward. 'The doctor is coming to examine your baby.'

'Why? What is wrong with it?'

'Nothing. We do routine checks on all new-borns.'

'Oh.'

Gwyneth tensed up as she watched the doctor feel all around the baby's head, as he peered at the face, looked in the ears and up the nose and shone a light in the eyes. Then he put a finger in its mouth and the pursed lips began to suck.

'If you'd undress her, please, nurse.'

When the doctor placed the stethoscope on its bare chest the baby howled in protest and Gwyneth felt a strange tingle in her nipples.

'Healthy pair of lungs there.' The doctor moved the stethoscope down to listen to the tummy, then straightened up.

Gwyneth relaxed, but he wasn't finished.

He held the baby's tiny hands, and pulled it up into a sitting position and the head flopped backwards.

Gwyneth gasped.

'Don't worry.' The nurse smiled. 'All babies' heads are a bit wobbly.'

The doctor lowered it down onto the bed and checked all the fingers were present, the same with the toes, something that Gwyneth had done many times. Holding a miniature knee in the palm of each hand, he held the legs together and pressed down then splayed them out, all the time feeling the hips with his fingers.

The baby kept wailing and Gwyneth felt milk spurt from her breasts. She folded her arms across her chest in an attempt to hide the damp patch seeping through the front of her nightdress.

'Nearly over now, sweetheart,' said the nurse stroking the baby's head with her forefinger.

The doctor picked up the baby and, with only a hand under its tummy, held it face down six inches above the bed. He ran the index finger of his other hand along the spine. 'That's fine. Just the Moro Reflex and then we're finished.' He turned the baby over and held it with one hand cupping its bottom, the other its head. 'Excellent,' he said as the baby's arms shot upwards when he slipped his hand from beneath the head before catching it again.

He handed the baby back to the nurse and turned to Gwyneth. 'Don't look so worried. Your baby's just fine.'

***

'First soap her all over.' The nurse rubbed suds all over the bony legs, the arms, the round tummy.

Gwyneth looked at the size of her baby then at her stomach and wondered how all that had fitted in there. The head was bigger than a large grapefruit. How on earth had that come out? No wonder there'd been so much pain.

The nurse picked up the now very slippery baby; the head flopped back bending its neck at the most alarming angle.

'You must be careful the water's not too hot tomorrow when you bath her on your own. Dip your elbow in first.'

Well that bit she could do – getting the temperature right – but lowering the baby into the water she wasn't sure she'd be able to do that without dropping it into the sink or cracking its head against the porcelain. Then, if she managed to get the baby into the water without mishap, there was still the danger of drowning. She could never do what the nurse was doing now: supporting it in the water with only one hand.

While it squirmed and wriggled, and kicked its legs, the nurse used her other hand to reach for a bit of cotton wool. 'Now first you clean her eyes. From the centre outwards. Don't want any infections, do we?' Then wash the face, then the hair.'

Gwyneth felt weak. She'd never manage all that. Thank goodness that it would be another three days before Valerie went back to *The House*. Valerie would help. Valerie would know what to do.

Valerie was in the next bed. She'd been there when the baby wouldn't finish its feed, wouldn't stop crying. She'd shown Gwyneth how to sit it up on her knee, lean it forward and support its chest with one hand, a thumb hooked under one armpit, her fingers clasping the other, how to use her other hand to rub its back and give it an occasional pat. A few minutes of this and a burp – very satisfying to both mother and baby – would emerge and the teat could go back in the baby's mouth. The gurgle as the last drop was sucked from the plastic bottle would indicate the feed was complete, and the baby would lie motionless, cheeks puffed out, milk dribbling from the corner of its mouth. With a drunken glaze over its eyes the baby would fall into a soporific sleep.

Valerie had taught her origami – a very necessary skill required when fitting a large square terry-towelling nappy to a round baby's bottom.

'Bring these two sides to the middle to make the shape of a kite. Now fold down the top then fold up the bottom, like this.' With one hand Valerie held both of the baby's feet and lifted the lower half up so she could slide the folded nappy into place. 'Now this bit is much narrower so you can pull it up between the legs. The top is wider so you can bring the sides around her tummy and pin it all together at the front.

'Pin it!' The safety-pin was two inches long and lethal.

'It'll be alright. Just make sure you put your hand behind the nappy. Then if the pin slips you jag your fingers not the baby. Here you try.'

Gwyneth struggled to get the point of the pin through many layers of towelling.

'Good job it's a girl you've got. Otherwise you'd be pinning his privates.'

'What if the pin comes undone?' asked Gwyneth.

'It won't if you do this.' Valerie pressed the pink safety catch into place.

There was no one to visit Gwyneth in hospital. Auntie Mair might have come if she'd phoned to tell her the news, but she didn't want Uncle George to find out where she was. Valerie, on the other hand, was never short of visitors: Brian, his mum and his little brothers, grandma, aunties and uncles. Once Valerie's mother had come and when they saw her enter the ward Brian's relatives had melted away.

Mrs Johnson's face was set in a fixed smile. She stared down at her new grandson but didn't reach into the cot to pick him up. Instead she brushed invisible crumbs from the armchair next to the bed and sat down. She spoke in low tones but Gwyneth could still hear what she'd said.

'Not long now. Just a few weeks, then you can come home and we can forget all about this unpleasant business.'

Valerie didn't answer. The baby began to cry so she got out of bed and picked him up.

'You mustn't do that. You'll spoil him.'

'There's a girl at *The House*; she carries her baby round with her all the time in a sling.'

'You don't want to take any notice of those girls up there. They're not like us.'

The baby's lip began to quiver and he started to wail. Valerie unbuttoned her nightdress and manoeuvred his mouth to her breast.

Her mother's body stiffened. 'But they told you. They told you not to do that. You'll get too attached.'

'You can't stop me. I'm sixteen now.'

'You're still my daughter and you'll do as you're told.'

Valerie didn't answer, just stared down at the baby and held him closer.

Eventually her mother got up. 'I'll have to go. Your father'll be home for his tea. Goodness knows what he's going to say.'

***

By Day Five, Valerie had gone back to *The House*, Paula had left a couple of days earlier and Gwyneth was now on her own. Visiting times were the worst. She read *Jackie* or pretended to be asleep as proud fathers and grandparents trooped in to see the other new arrivals and cast pitying glances in her direction.

'How are you, Gwyneth?'

A familiar turquoise hat was the first thing Gwyneth saw when she opened her eyes.

'She's lovely, dear,' said Miss M as she peered into the cot at the end of the bed. 'What are you going to call her?'

'Nothing. I'm not going to call it anything. I'm giving it away, so what's the point. They'll choose another name anyway.' Gwyneth sniffed and wiped a tear from the corner of her eye with her forefinger.

'But you'll be looking after her for the next few weeks. You can't go on calling her it.'

'Don't you understand. I don't want to look after it. I want to go home.'

'Well, I suppose I could try and get her fostered, but it means she'll just be getting to know you, to recognise your voice, then it'll be a foster mum for a couple of weeks, then she'll move on again. Too much chopping and changing isn't good for babies.'

'But what about me? Nobody thinks about what's good for me.'

'You've had a hard time, haven't you, dear?'

Miss M had only once asked about the baby's father. When she realised any of her girls didn't want to tell her, she never asked again. Perhaps this was why Gwyneth started to explain.

'I didn't know, see. I didn't know.' Gwyneth shook her head and twisted the sheet in her fingers. 'Only when I told Mam I was expecting and she asked who was the father. That was when I found out.'

'Found out what, dear?'

Gwyneth stared at the large black numbers on the clock hung above the door to the nursery at the far end of the ward. 'I promised Mam I wouldn't tell.'

'It's alright, dear, you don't have to tell me if you don't want to, but sometimes it helps to get things off your chest.'

After a long pause the words came out in a rush. 'Geraint, the baby's father, is my half-brother.' Gwyneth stared at Miss M trying to judge from her face what her reaction would be.

But Miss M's face didn't register shock, disgust or any of the emotions she'd expected. This middle-aged spinster took it all in her stride, just nodded sympathetically, reached out and placed her hand over Gwyneth's.

'It was my Dad, see. Carrying on with this woman he was. Mam didn't find out until the woman died having his baby. Dad asked if she'd take in his baby, but Mam said no 'cause she was expecting me. So, Geraint was brought up by his Nan, a right old witch she was. No one dared ask who was Geraint's father.'

'So only your mother knows about this?'

'Yes.' Her secret was out and the tears that Gwyneth had held back for so long streamed down her face. 'Mam said we'd have to get rid of it, so we tried with a rubber tube, water and carbolic soap, but it didn't work. I was too far gone, see.'

Miss M passed Gwyneth a neatly folded, embroidered handkerchief.

'Then Mam said I couldn't stay at home or it would all come out. Everyone would see the baby wasn't normal. Like with the family who had the farm over by Holyhead. The girl there had a baby. It didn't look right, and simple it was. Everyone said it was fathered by her brother.' She stopped, aware that she was raising her voice, but the other women on the ward had looked away and were now talking to their visitors.

Miss M put her arm round Gwyneth's shoulders. 'But it's not the same. You and Geraint had different mothers and anyway it doesn't always happen that there's something wrong with the baby. Miss M stood up and peeped into the cot. 'Look, she's awake. Can I pick her up?'

Gwyneth shrugged. 'If you like.'

CHAPTER 6

"Island of Dreams"
The Seekers 1966

Two buckets. That's what you need.'

'What?'

Before her baby was born Gwyneth had seen mums carrying the things they needed for their babies, but hadn't taken any notice. Then it had been part of a future she couldn't accept would happen to her.

Now it had: Gwyneth was back at *The House* and Miss M was showing her the ropes or more precisely telling her *The House Rules for Mums*. They were standing in what had once been the scullery where two rusty twin-tub washing machines stood alongside a pair of chipped porcelain sinks.

'The green bucket you keep in here. And it's best you write your name on it. Saves any arguments.'

Gwyneth frowned.

'When you take off the nappy you soak it in this bucket in water and some of that.' Miss M indicated the tubs of *Napisan* stacked against the wall. 'If it's soiled rinse it in the toilet first. Most of the girls hate doing that, but you must.'

'Brought up on a farm I was. A bit of shit don't bother me.'

Miss M raised her eyebrows. 'Quite so, but anyway, if you use one of these …' She pulled a small rectangle of stretchy material from among the other tiny garments hanging on a wooden clothes-airer suspended from the ceiling. '… a nappy liner, it's much easier, better for baby's skin too. Every two days, without fail, you must rinse off the nappies. Then wash them. The washing machine's not working isn't an excuse. There's still the sink and a spin dryer over there.'

Gwyneth followed Miss M back through the kitchen and across the passage into the nursery. Once a library, all four walls were lined from floor to ceiling with dark wooden shelves, but the books had gone, replaced by rows of bottles: large brown bottles of Milton, small round bottles of concentrated orange juice, tall thin bottles of cod liver oil.

Miss M pointed to a trestle table beneath shelves packed with blue and grey boxes with NDM in large letters on the front. 'You make the baby's feeds here. Everyone uses National Dried Milk.' Miss M smiled at Paula who was standing at the table dipping a scoop into one of the boxes and levelling off the yellowish powder with a knife before tipping it into one of the six baby's bottles lined up in front of her. 'Are you alright, dear?'

Paula didn't reply at once but repeated the process once more before turning around. Her face was grey and there were black circles under her eyes.

'Sorry, I was countin.'

'You look very tired, dear.'

'Gina woke up at half past eleven. It was gone half past one when she settled, then she was screaming again at five.' Paula turned to face Gwyneth. 'It's a doddle at Florrie's. All bottle-fed babies off to the nursery at nine to give the night staff something to do. Now it's you that's gorra do the night feeds. Wait until you've been back as long as I have. You'll be knackered.'

'Well try and get some rest, dear, while baby's asleep.'

'You're jokin'. Paula put the bottles on the window sill to cool. 'I've still got the nappies to do.'

Two buckets you told me now just?'

'Ah. Yes, Gwyneth.' Miss M moved over to where baby baths with stands, bouncy chairs and buckets were stacked against the wall. She picked up a yellow bucket. 'This is for sterilizing the bottles and teats. Now remember yellow for bottles, green for nappies. It's very important you don't get them mixed up.'

Gwyneth looked over at Paula and raised her eyebrows.

Miss M didn't notice as she had already moved on to the far side of the room. 'Ours are the best dressed babies in the district,' she said pointing to the bookshelves that lined the walls. 'We have lots of clothes, kindly donated by church members whose babies have grown up.' Neat hand-written labels were stuck beneath piles of vests, sleep-suits, dungarees, rompers, tiny dresses, suits, mittens, bonnets and bootees. Miss M beckoned Gwyneth over. 'Now find a pretty dress and something nice and warm to go on top then go and fetch Eirlys - such a lovely name. I'm so pleased you chose it.'

'She's sleeping.'

'Well you know what Nurse Harding says.' Miss M nodded towards the window through which they could see prams parked in a line on the overgrown lawn. 'Babies need fresh air.'

As Gwyneth bent over Eirlys's cot, she muttered, 'There is crazy these English are. December it is … and freezing.'

The baby's eyelids flickered; her brow furrowed as if to say: Why am I here? What's this all about? This baby so vulnerable, so dependent on others. With one hand under the baby's bottom, the other supporting her head, Gwyneth lifted her up and laid her on the changing mat. She prised apart the poppers on the inside leg of the sleep-suit, pulled off the plastic pants then removed the nappy. Free of the restriction of clothing, the baby flexed both legs and fanned out her toes. As she put on a clean nappy, Gwyneth looked down at the snub nose, the puckered mouth with a sucking blister on the top lip, the miniature ears and thought, *she's just perfect*. She hadn't been prepared for this.

Did Eirlys look like Geraint? Maybe the eyes were the same, but then all babies' eyes were blue. Gently she eased the sleep-suit over the baby's head. Geraint would never know he had a daughter. Did she love Geraint? She thought so at the time; that's why she'd gone all the way with him. Not just once like some of the girls here claimed. It wasn't just Geraint who'd wanted it, she did too. But she hadn't wanted a baby. They'd been careful, used a French letter. She couldn't understand how it had happened. It wasn't fair.

Gwyneth lifted the tiny head to put on the frilly pink and white dress then bent the flailing arms to go through the sleeves. At first, she'd been frightened of breaking the delicate limbs but not now. She lifted the baby to her chest to do up the buttons down the back and felt the small body nestle into her.

'*O Cariad. Cariad bach.*' Tears trickled down Gwyneth's cheeks.

No, Gwyneth told herself. No. There was no way she was keeping this baby. For six weeks she'd do everything she could for Eirlys, but after that she'd have a new name, she'd belong to someone else, to a family who could give her more than she could, take her to live somewhere where no one would point the finger and call her a bastard or keep asking who her father was.

'What are you doing?' Valerie stood in the doorway.

'Just putting this on.'

'Here, I'll do it.'

'I can manage.'

When Eirlys was enveloped in a fluffy coat that extended way beyond her toes where it folded over and buttoned up into a sleeping bag, they took her downstairs. Valerie led the way to the dilapidated conservatory where the prams were kept. Most were of the coach-built variety, with bicycle-sized wheels; so many in such a poor state of repair that Gwyneth suspected that, rather than an act of charity, bringing them here was a way to get rid of them.

'Brian and I are getting one of those.' Valerie pointed to a much lower and squarish type of pram with smaller wheels 'A carrycot and transporter. But a new one of course.'

They selected what must have once been a very elegant model: navy blue with Silver Cross autographed on the side, the enormous wheels now rusty, with spokes missing. Valerie wiped the interior with a cloth then arranged the blankets and pillows and Gwyneth laid Eirlys down. They raised the hood, clipped on the apron so there was only a small aperture through which to peep at the baby. Eirlys gazed back at the two girls still with an expression of utter confusion. Gwyneth wheeled the pram out to join the others.

'How long do we have to leave them out here?'

'Well, Nurse Harding comes out to check they're all here at about eleven. After that she doesn't notice if a couple of us bring them back inside.'

***

'I gor it.' Paula stood in the nursery doorway, looking much happier than she had in the three and a half weeks since her baby was born.

Gwyneth and Valerie were bathing their babies. Gina

was in a reclining baby chair looking on.

Paula knelt down and unclipped the safety-strap. With hands encircling the tiny chest she lifted her baby out of the chair, then raised her above her head and whirled her round. 'I gor the job. Isn't your Mam clever?'

'What job?' asked Gwyneth staring at the knee-high boots and a bright orange mini-skirt she was sure she hadn't seen Paula wearing before. 'You didn't say anything about a job when you asked us to look after Gina.'

'Well, I didn't tell you in case I didn't ger it.'

'So where is it?'

'The fashion department at Harrods.'

'Didn't you need references?'

'Yea, course I did.'

'So, where did you say you'd been for the last six months?'

'Well Susan sorted that fore she left. Her cousin has a boutique in the Kings Road. She wrote one for us.'

'But you never worked there.'

'I know but in Liverpool I did work in John Lewis. I told them that too.'

'But that was in haberdashery.'

When at tea-time, Paula told everyone the good news, Miss M said that was wonderful and asked when her new job began. Paula replied that she started full time after Christmas, but hesitated before adding that she had also agreed to work one day a week until then, beginning this coming Saturday.

'When you agreed to do that, what were you planning to do about Gina? 'asked Miss M.

'Thought Valerie might …'

'That's not fair,' said Miss M. 'She's got a baby of her

own to look after.'

'I don't mind,' said Valerie.

'No, Nurse Harding and I will do it.'

'I'm afraid I can't. I've booked the next two Saturdays off.'

A questioning frown crossed Miss M face as she looked at her colleague at the far end of the table, then she turned to her left. 'Then I'm sure one of our Ladies in Waiting will help.

'I will,' said Christine.

'Me too,' said another of the pregnant girls. 'Give me some practice.'

'Thank you both,' said Miss M and then turned to Paula. 'You'll have to get on with it now. Find yourself somewhere to live, someone to look after Gina while you're at work.'

At noon for the next three days Paula was there, standing outside the newsagent with Gina in the pram. As soon as the *Evening Standard* arrived, she'd hurry back up the hill to *The House*. Holding a bottle in the baby's mouth, she'd scan down the *Accommodation to Let* column and mark possibles in biro: possibles needed to be less than five pounds a week otherwise after paying rent, bills, food and a childminder there'd be nothing left.

When Gina was fed and changed, she'd put her in a carrycot and ease it down into the transporter, which she'd push round and round the garden. Once the baby was asleep, she'd bring the carrycot back into the nursery and get one of the girls to listen out, before rushing off, promising to be back by five.

'Any luck?' asked Gwyneth when she came back on the Wednesday.

'There was one, but it was just the one room with a Baby

Belling in the corner and share a bathroom.'

On Thursday the answer was: 'Nothin', just this bed-sit with a gas ring, two bus rides from work, but I was gonna take it. Then I told the landlady I had a baby and she said it was already taken. How could it be? Did she think I was stupid or what?'

On Friday Paula flopped onto the settee. 'Couldn't believe it – my own bathroom and a separate bedroom. Told the landlord, a fellar in his forties wearing flares and winkle-pickers, that I didn't have a lorra cash because I had a baby and he actually reduced the rent.'

Gwyneth raised her eyebrows. 'Didn't take it, did you?'

'I was gonna. Then he asked did I ger out much? Said maybe sometime he could take me and Gina for a drive in the country.'

It was before seven when Paula left to work her first Saturday shift at Harrods; it would take more than an hour and a half on the bus to Knightsbridge. Baby Gina was asleep when she left, but woke up soon after Paula crept out the front door. When the other girls came down Miss M was in the nursery giving the very disgruntled baby a bottle. Throughout breakfast Gina howled.

Christine took over during the morning and ended up shushing the baby in her arms and jiggling her up and down. When Gina finally stopped crying and went to sleep, she put her in a pram and parked it outside at the end of the line and came to join the other girls in the sitting room.

'Like babies do you, Christine?' asked Gwyneth.

'Never looked after one before, but I did child care at school, 'cause I wasn't clever enough to do science.'

'Yes, I remember at our school the girls from 5C used to practice bathing dolls.'

'We did other things too,' said Christine. 'Had these pictures and you had to draw a circle round the things that weren't safe like a bottle of pills with no top on or an iron still plugged in. I liked doing that.'

Valerie came in with the post. 'One for you, Christine. From the DHSS, I think. And one for Paula. It's got an Italian stamp. Do you think it's from Gino? Must be. She's written him lots of letters.' Valerie propped it up on the mantelpiece and then looked over to Christine. 'Aren't you going to open yours?'

'I'll read it later,' said Christine.

Christine gave Gina her six o' clock feed, changed her nappy then asked Valerie what time Paula had said she'd be back.

'Seven at the latest,' said Valerie.

By half past Paula still hadn't arrived, so Miss M decided it was well past a baby's bedtime and took Gina upstairs.

When Miss M still hadn't come down over an hour later, Gwyneth went up to Paula's room, knocked gently then pushed open the door. Miss M, the baby in her arms, was pacing up and down, looking out through the attic window to the driveway below. She turned around, relief on her face, but seeing Gwyneth standing in the doorway it turned to concern. 'Oh, I thought you were Paula.'

'No. There is a worry it is. Will we call the police?'

'She's probably just got held up in all this Christmas traffic. We'll wait a bit longer.' said Miss M raising her voice to be heard above Gina's screams. 'Perhaps you could ask Valerie to come up, see if she can settle Gina. She's so good with the little ones.'

Valerie had Gina tucked up and sound asleep by ten, but Paula still wasn't home. Miss M told the girls to go to bed and leave things to her. She would find Paula. But no one at *The House* could get to sleep that night.

At one-thirty the girls heard footsteps on the gravel, the jangle of the bell, then the front door open and close. They crept out of their rooms onto the landings to peer over the banister. Below them was Paula's beehive hairdo sprinkled with snow and Miss M's tight perm encased in a pink hairnet.

'Well, Paula,' said Miss M. 'Go to bed now. We'll speak in the morning.'

After morning prayers Paula stayed behind in Miss M's office. When she emerged, half an hour later, the girls crowded around.

'Where were you last night?'

'Ar a party with the girls from the shoe department. It was fab. You should have seen the talent.'

'We were worried. You should have rung to let us know.'

'Whar, and have Miss M tell me to come home.'

'Was she very angry?'

'Not really. Just told me to think carefully about what I'm going to do. Did I wanna be a mother to Gina or did I wanna go to parties 'cause I couldn't do both.'

'Oh! there's a letter for you.' Valerie pointed to the envelope with the Italian stamp propped up on the mantelpiece.

Paula tore it open and began to read.

'Is it from Gino?' asked Valerie.

The girls watched in silence as Paula sank down into an armchair and turned the single sheet over and dropped it into her lap.

'What is it, then?' asked Gwyneth.

It was several minutes before she replied. 'He's gonna

marry an Italian girl. Says not to write no more. I can't prove the baby is his.'

That night, as usual, when she went to bed Gwyneth took two bottles upstairs and stood them on the sill outside the window to keep cool. She thought of the long, wearisome hours that lay ahead. Paula was right. It had been a doddle at Florrie's: nurses to make up the bottles, to give the night feeds while mothers got eight hours undisturbed sleep. One of the bottles on the window sill was for the two o'clock feed the other for six o'clock.

But here back at *The House*, it didn't work out like that. Eirlys woke up just after midnight. At first it was just the odd whimper: a combination of a cough and a hiccup. Gwyneth tried to block out the sound by covering her ears with the pillow, but the cries became louder and more persistent. There would be the odd pause for breath then it would start up again, like a car engine being revved up at the start of a race or a saw being pulled and pushed back and forth, grating its way through a tree trunk. Gwyneth got out of bed, switched on the light and looked into the cot. Eirlys's face was bright red and furious, her eyes screwed up into slits, her mouth wide open.

Gwyneth picked up the screaming infant. '*Hisht, hisht.* You will wake the whole house, indeed you will.'

Eventually Eirlys calmed down enough to take her two o'clock bottle, but when it was finished, she showed no signs of going to sleep. At half past three, mother and baby dozed off, side by side on the bed. At five o'clock, Eirlys was once again demanding food.

Gwyneth slept through the "Getting up" bell and the "Breakfast" bell and only woke up when someone shook her.

'It's me. Valerie. Miss M sent me to see if you're alright.'

'Go away. Leave me alone.'

Eirlys, lying on the bed beside her, began to whimper again.

Gwyneth opened her eyes. 'I can't do this.'

CHAPTER 7

"Love's just a Broken Heart"
Cilla Black 1966

Nurse Harding said Eirlys had colic. That's why, when she was laid down in her cot, she squirmed, drew up her knees and screamed. Gwyneth began to recognise the signs of wind: a blueish tinge round the mouth along with the slight upward curl of the lips and wide staring eyes. Some of the mothers liked to think that their babies were smiling at them. Valerie insisted that in his book Dr Spock said that babies couldn't focus, didn't recognise a face and definitely couldn't smile until they were at least six weeks old. By then the girls would have given them away.

Now Gwyneth knew what to do. She sat Eirlys on her knee, gave her a teaspoon of gripe water then leant her forward, so the baby's chin was resting on her chest, and rubbed her back. After a while the tiny body would erupt in a series of burps, before she relaxed, gave a yawn and fell asleep. Gwyneth laid Eirlys in her cot. As she watched her sleep, Gwyneth's heart went out to her daughter: she wanted to take care of her, protect her, watch her grow up. Then her head would take over and tell her this was impossible: Where would they live? What would they live on? How would she cope with a toddler, a teenager? By the time her child had grown up, she herself would be too old to do all the things she had planned for her life. No, there was no option. Eirlys must be adopted. Tomorrow she would go with Miss M to the adoption agency.

Miss M had explained that this first appointment was so the adoption people could meet her and the baby, have a chat, ask her a few questions and fill in the forms. This would give them some background to help them find the most suitable parents.

But what could she tell them about Eirlys's background? Mam had warned her over and over again not to tell anyone that the father of her baby was her half-brother. No one would want a baby born out of incest.

Apart from her mother, Miss M was the only person who knew. If only she hadn't told Miss M. At Florrie's, when her emotions were swinging this way and that, she had looked into Miss M's eyes and thought this is someone who'll understand, who'll keep a secret. And Gwyneth was sure she would, if it wasn't for the fact that it was Miss M who would go with her to the agency. Miss M, who said that it was always best to tell the truth.

Next morning after breakfast she knocked on the office door.

'Come in, Gwyneth. This must be a hard day for you. Not having second thoughts, are you?'

Gwyneth shook her head, 'You know, in the hospital I told you about Eirlys's father?'

'I'm not sure I remember, dear. Anyway, you never told me his name.'

'Oh.' Gwyneth stared at Miss M. She wasn't old, not prone to lapses of memory.

'His name's not on the birth certificate.'

'No.'

'Then if they ask you about him at the adoption agency, it might be best to say you don't know his name. It happened at a party. You'd had too much to drink.'

'But what will they think of me?'

'It doesn't matter what they think of you, dear. All that matters is what they think about the baby.' Miss M put her hand over Gwyneth's. 'No need to make people think there might be a problem, or they'll look for signs that aren't there. Remember what the doctor said: Eirlys is perfect.'

The adoption agency was above a boutique at the top of two flights of very narrow stairs. The name *Families Forever* was imprinted in a semicircle above a heart on the opaque glass on the door to the office. Two women rose to greet Gwyneth and Miss M and both cooed over Eirlys.

'Do you think she might have red hair?' asked the older woman with long, grey hair arranged in a bun on top of her head.

The other woman with the pink rinse and bright red lipstick studied the sparse down on the baby's head and said. 'No red-heads in your family are there?'

'I don't think so.' As Gwyneth sat down on a chair in front of a large polished desk, Eirlys made a grunting sound and stirred so she held the baby closer to her chest and began to rock backwards and forward.

Miss M pulled up another chair and handed over the birth certificate.

The two women now ensconced behind their desk exchanged glances when they saw the blank space.

'Is there anything you can tell us about the father?'

Gwyneth shook her head.

They looked at Miss M, who said, 'Sometimes unfortunate things happen to the nicest of girls.'

'Well she's such a sweet little thing, I'm sure we can find her a suitable family.' The younger woman took a blank card from a drawer. 'Just need to take a few details. Your father, what's his job?'

Gwyneth frowned trying to decide why this was relevant. 'He's a farmer.'

'And what's your religion?'

'Baptist.'

Did you pass your eleven plus?'

'Yes, I went to the grammar school.'

'Did you get any GCEs?'

'Eight and three A levels.'

'What hobbies do you have?'

'Well, I go swimming. I like reading.'

'And as far as you know there are no medical problems or illnesses that run in the family?'

Gwyneth shook her head.

When the questions were over, the older woman looked at the calendar. 'She'll be six weeks on the ninth of January. I think we'll probably be able to arrange the handover sometime the following week.'

'What is all this about red hair?' Gwyneth asked Miss M on the bus home.

'It can be a mistake to place a red-headed baby with a family where there are no relatives with red hair.'

'Oh, I see! And all those other questions. What were they for?'

'They like to match the new parents as closely as possible with the birth family to give the babies the best possible start in life.'

'So, everyone will think she is their baby, is it?' Gwyneth blinked back the tears and stared out of the window. She looked down at Eirlys asleep in her arms and counted the days they'd still have together, at the most 28. Up until now it had seemed an eternity to wait until she was free to go back to her former life, but now it seemed like no time at all.

***

The following morning Gwyneth was on her way upstairs with a pile of clean nappies when she heard the doorbell jangle and, being the nearest, she turned, crossed the hall and opened the front door. She'd only seen the woman standing at the top of the steps once before and that had been when she was still on the ward at Florrie's. However, there are some people you never forget: the fur coat, the permed hair rising from her forehead to curl round at the sides and fall into rigidly set waves at the back. Why did women of that age think that by rinsing it pink no one would realise their roots were turning grey?

'Oh hello, Mrs Johnson. Come in.' Gwyneth led the way down the hall. 'I'll tell Valerie you're here, get her to bring Brian down.'

'Brian! What's he doing upstairs?'

'No, not Brian. The baby I mean, your grandson.'

'No, tell her to leave the baby where it is. It's her I've come to see.'

Gwyneth left Mrs Johnson on the visitor's settee just inside the sitting room, and went to fetch Valerie.

'I'm not coming down.'

'There is silly you are. You must tell your mother you want to keep your baby.'

'She knows that.'

'Only saying I was, that she might change her mind.'

Valerie stared out of the attic window. 'OK, but don't leave me alone with her.'

The two girls went downstairs and into the sitting room together. Valerie sat at the opposite end of the settee from her mother, and Gwyneth joined the other girls around the gas fire at the far end of the room. As the argument between mother and daughter escalated, the other girls glanced at each other and continued to turn the pages of *Jackie* and click their knitting needles.

'Impossible. You can't go and live with his family. They're common: milk bottles on the table at meal times, all those children with runny noses and nits.'

Valerie's voice rose even louder, 'But if I go to live with them, I can keep Brian.'

'Fancy calling the baby after that waster! And I've told you before. There's no way you can keep him. You have to go back to school after Christmas.'

'Brian's mum will look after him.'

'I've told you, Valerie. It's out of the question.'

Mrs Johnson stood up and fastened her coat. 'I'm going to see Miss M now … about the adoption.'

'No, Mum, you can't make me, you can't.'

Valerie shut herself in her room for the rest of the day. After she'd shown Mrs Johnson out, Miss M went upstairs.

Valerie was sitting on the floor with her back pressed against the door and wouldn't let anyone in, just yelled, 'You're on her side. You don't want me and Brian to keep our baby.'

'That's not true,' said Miss M. 'But we can't sort it out by shouting at each other through this door. Can we?'

'Miss M, Miss M.' Gwyneth stopped on the first-floor landing to catch her breath. 'There's a man at the door with a Christmas tree.'

'I'm coming.' Miss M turned and spoke to the closed door. 'I'm going downstairs now, Valerie. When you come down, we'll talk about it.'

The girls decided the best place for the tree was in the sitting room in the alcove where Nina did the ironing. Gwyneth and two of the other mums dragged the tree down the hall.

'A present from the Ladies on the Committee,' said Miss M as they held it upright in a large tin bath while the other girls packed earth and stones round the trunk to stop it falling over.

'My mum never bought us a Christmas tree,' said Christine.

'Well then, dear, you must be in charge of decorating this one. There's some baubles and some tinsel in there.' Miss M pointed to two cardboard boxes. 'The other girls will help. One of the mums will put the angel on the top. Don't you go standing on a chair, Christine. Don't want you going into labour just yet.'

Christine had already started to open the boxes, pulling out silver tinsel and gazing in child-like wonder at the red and green baubles.

'We'll put the lights on first,' said Paula as she began to unravel the tangle of flex and coloured bulbs.

There were plenty of volunteers to decorate the tree, so Gwyneth joined the girls sitting around the table and helped to make paper-chains.

Nina had stuck a red candle into a hole she'd made in the centre of half a raw potato covered with tinfoil. She now added a white bow and sprigs of holly which she'd sprinkled with glitter. She leant back in her chair and surveyed her handiwork. 'For Christmas Day on the table. Do you like?'

Gwyneth added another link to her paper-chain and looked up. 'Mam used to make them.'

'It is pity I am not here when you light it,' sighed Nina.

'Why, when are you going?' asked Gwyneth.

'Tomorrow.'

'But that's just four days before Christmas.'

'I like to stay for Christmas here, but it is not possible.'

'Where are you going?'

'Miss M, she knows this place for girls with babies. You have one room where you must cook and sleep.'

'A bed-sitter?'

'When I get job the lady who lives there will look after baby.'

'But Nina, you'll never be able to leave him with somebody else.'

Nina stroked the baby's head as he slept in the sling tied around her chest. 'There is nothing else to do. The Ladies on the Committee they say I cannot stay here for longer.'

The following morning cook sorted out some pots and pans, crockery and cutlery that she swore were no longer needed. Miss M found some unwanted sheets, pillow cases and blankets then ordered a taxi to take Nina, her baby and her few possessions to the bed-sit.

'I thank you for everything. I will miss you all too much.'

'We'll miss you, Nina,' said Miss M.

'Who'll sing the hymns and do the ironing?' asked Paula.

'Come back and see us, mind.' said Gwyneth.

'I try,' said Nina as she supported her baby's head and bent down to get into the taxi.

As the girls stood on the steps waving, the postman came up the drive and handed over a package. It was addressed to Paula, Gwyneth and Valerie.

Inside were three envelopes addressed to each of the girls.

Gwyneth tore hers open first. 'What is this then? A

Christmas card, from Susan.'

Valerie peeled back the flap of the envelope. 'Mine's the same, and a photo. It's of us! The one Nina took on the day Susan left.'

Paula, who was still holding the package, gave it a shake and a letter fell out. She picked it up and began to read it out loud.

Dear Paula, Valerie and Gwyneth,

I guess you have all had your babies by now. I often think about you and wonder how you are getting on. I have been home for more than a month now and this house seems very empty and lonely. While I was at The House I couldn't wait to get away, for it all to be over, but now I miss you all. No one talks about where I've been for the last three months. When I mention my baby, father says that it's over, it's a part of my life I must forget and in time I'll come to believe it never happened. But what does he know? Nothing like this has ever happened to him. I won't forget.

Mother keeps trying to cheer me up and invites what she calls eligible young men round to dinner. But they are all real bores. I can't imagine how she thinks I would want to be seen out with any of them.

When I was at The House, you were like the sisters I'd never had. It's always only been me and Mother and Father. I would like to keep in touch, but then people are always saying that and never do. So, in case we don't see each other in the coming years I am sending each of you a print of the photo taken on the day that I left. On the back is a place, a date and time in December 1987. By then all our babies will be twenty-one.

See you there.

Love

Susan.

There is nonsense for you,' said Gwyneth. 'Who knows

where we will be then.'

'Well, I think it's a nice idea,' said Valerie.

'You won't if they make you give up your baby.'

'They can't do that. I won't let them.'

'What do you think, Paula?'

'Well, in the beginning I thought Susan was a right stuck up little bitch. But when yer got to know her she wasn't that bad. Do you know what she did? One day she said she liked my dress, you know, the one with the Peter Pan collar. When I said I'd gor it out of a catalogue and hadn't finished paying it off, she gave me five quid, just like that.'

'Well, she could afford it.'

'I know, but she didn't have to give me the money, did she?'

'So, have you paid it all off?'

'Well no, the old biddy who does the catalogue lives in the flat above where Gino and I used to stay. Susan gave me the money the day that I thought I was in labour. Couldn't take the money to her then, could I? What if me waters had broken on the bus?'

Gwyneth had an image in her mind of Paula putting a new album by the Rolling Stones on the record player around that time. She had wondered then how Paula, who claimed she had no money, could afford to buy the *Aftermath* LP. But Gwyneth was learning that when you lived in such close quarters with so many other girls there were things that it was often best not to mention. She went up to her room, put the photograph in the inside pocket of her suitcase and pushed it back under the bed. She stood the Christmas card up on the mantelpiece and wondered if this year there would be any others to put alongside it.

CHAPTER 8

"Tomorrow never knows"
The Beatles 1966

Cook wrote instructions about the last-minute preparations for Christmas. She would have liked to stop and cook the dinner herself, but she was proud grandma to four boys and seven girls, aged three months to thirteen years. She made no secret of the fact that two of them had been "surprises" and hastened a wedding, in hindsight not always the best solution! Christmas was a time for families she said and wiped away a tear with her apron; it was a crying shame that the girls at *The House* would not see their mothers and fathers, their brothers and sisters this year.

The pudding was stirred and liberally sprinkled with sixpences, the Christmas cake baked, brandied, marzipanned and iced, the mince pies dusted with icing sugar. But by lunchtime on Christmas Eve there was still no turkey. The delivery boy's bike had a puncture. It would be with them by four at the latest. Cook was very sorry but she couldn't stay any longer: the family were gathering at Milton Keynes and she had a train to catch. Miss M said it wasn't a problem; she was sure she could manage to draw the turkey and as for everything else she would supervise the girls and make sure that the Christmas cooking instructions were followed to the letter.

As the afternoon wore on, Miss M began to look peaky and wore a shawl draped over her cardigan. Nurse Harding diagnosed influenza and sent her to bed with two aspirins.

But who's gonna draw the turkey?' asked Paula.

'It's all right,' said Christine. 'I'll do it.'

The other girls stared. 'How d'you know how to do it? You said you'd never had Christmas dinner before.'

'Saw it on the TV. Fanny Craddock.'

So, when the turkey arrived Christine chopped off its head and put her fingers down through its neck to loosen its innards, while the other girls averted their eyes. Then she turned it round to make a slit at the bottom end and put her hand inside to draw out a slippery mass of lungs, liver and guts, while the girls who had not yet given birth, and some of those who had, fled from the kitchen.

After tea Christine supervised the wrapping of the sausage pigs in their streaky-bacon blankets, the mixing of stuffing. The girls doing the potatoes consulted her about how many they should peel. She told Gwyneth that cutting a cross in the stalk of the Brussels sprouts would make them cook quicker, and that battens rather than slices was the modern way to cut carrots. Miss M, who'd come downstairs to check everything was OK, returned to her sick bed with a hot toddy, leaving all advance preparations in Christine's capable hands.

After the babies were settled, the mums joined the Ladies in Waiting in the circle around the gas fire. Apart from the Christmas tree in the alcove, paper chains looped round the picture rail and Franky and Bruce's Christmas Show on the tele, it was no different from any other evening.

'So excited my little sister will be, leaving a carrot for Rudolph, hanging up her stocking,' said Gwyneth.

'I think we should do that,' said Christine.

'What, leave a carrot for Rudolf?'

'No, silly. Hang up our stockings.'

'And who's going to fill them? Is Miss M going to creep about dressed in a red suit with a white beard?

'If she crept in my room and woke my baby there'd be trouble.'

'And what would she put in the stockings? Isn't as if we've got lots of prezzies.'

All eyes turned to the parcels beneath the Christmas tree. Some of the girls' parents had sent presents, but not all. Paula's hadn't because they didn't know where she was. Christine's mum probably didn't realise it was Christmas. So, any parcels from home were taken straight upstairs to be opened in private on Christmas morning. This left just thirty-six parcels: eighteen all the same shape, but wrapped in different coloured festive paper; on the gift tags were the girls' names and the words: *With love Miss M*. Then there were another eighteen assorted parcels, one for each girl from one of the others. This had all been arranged weeks ago. Miss M had explained that everyone should be "saving the pennies" for the day they left *The House*. And it wasn't fair if some girls got lots of presents, while those who had just arrived got hardly any. Each girl would buy for just one of the other girls; which one would be decided by drawing names out of a hat. Gwyneth had to buy for the girl – no, woman because she must be in her late twenties - who kept herself to herself; rumour had it that this was her second illegitimate baby. Not knowing what to buy her, Gwyneth had gone to Boots and bought talc and bath salts.

The only one so excited that she couldn't sleep on Christmas Eve was Christine. The others still awake were either pacing the floor shushing their babies, or lying in bed worrying about what the New Year might bring.

***

The aroma of roast turkey wafted up the stairs as the girls came down to breakfast. The bird weighed in at twenty pounds and Gwyneth had worked out that, at twenty minutes to the pound and twenty minutes over, it would take seven hours to cook. Christine had got up to wrap it in its waistcoat of raw pastry to stop the breast over-browning, before putting it in the oven at five-thirty.

Miss M wasn't at breakfast. Nurse Harding said she still wasn't well, but she would be down for the present-opening and hopefully stay up until after Christmas dinner.

Normally babies were confined to their mums' bedrooms, the nursery, or the garden for their morning airing. The only time they were allowed in the sitting room was when their mums entertained visitors on the settees just inside the door. Miss M had justified these rules with the words: 'babies needed routine, peace and quiet and not too much excitement.' Paula had murmured 'There's not much excitement goes on in our sitting room.'

However, the Ladies on the Committee did make an exception on Christmas Day: after all, for most of the girls this would be the only Christmas they would share with their babies. For days beforehand, the girls had rummaged through the baby clothes on the nursery bookshelves, bagging the best for their baby to wear on this special day. So, at ten o'clock all the babies arrived dressed in pink frilly dresses and smart blue romper suits. Instead of a cold hour in the garden, they slept in their mum's laps or waved their arms and kicked their legs as they lay on the sitting room carpet.

The present opening didn't take long. Those from family had already been opened by the girls on their own in their rooms. Gwyneth's mum had sent her a Fair Isle hat, scarf and gloves that must have taken ages to knit. Valerie's parents had sent her a Barbie doll which she'd thrown in the bin.

Miss M had bought everyone a diary. Valerie flipped through the pages until she came to November, then took out the pencil.

'What you writing?' asked Gwyneth.

'Baby Brian's birthday 22nd November.'

Gwyneth wanted to say that she didn't need to write it down. No mother would ever forget the day her baby was born. But she kept her mouth shut.

'Oh no.' Christine leapt to her feet. 'The pudding. I forgot the pudding. Fanny said it needed to steam for at least three hours.'

Paula and Gwyneth followed her into the kitchen.

'Don't worry. It's only half-past ten,' said Gwyneth.

Paula stopped beside the stove and wrinkled her nose at a pan of murky liquid on the hob. A pinkish-brown scum was boiling away on the surface. 'Whar's at?'

'The giblets from inside the turkey.'

'I'm nor eating that!'

'You don't eat them. It's the stock for the gravy.' said Christine.

'Our mam uses Bisto,'said Paula.

When they'd boiled the kettle and filled the steamer and Christine had checked everything else, they returned to the sitting room.

'Here's yours.' Valerie handed the three girls their presents.

Christine tore off the paper and was over the moon with a box of Quality Street. Paula was also delighted with her prezzie. She wore the red plastic chandelier earrings for the rest of the day.

Gwyneth could tell what her present was from the shape. Written on the label in uneven letters were the words: *To Gwinith frum Christine.* With a fixed smile on her face, determined to look pleased whatever the book might turn out to be, Gwyneth removed the wrapping. '*The Chrysalids.* How did you know I like John Wyndham?'

Christine beamed. 'I asked Paula. She helped me.'

A couple of the mums had bought presents for their babies. Valerie was one of them. She knelt on the floor with baby Brian propped up between her knees and ripped off the paper she'd carefully wrapped round the plastic toy the night before. 'Look Brian,' she said pressing a green button. A clown with an exaggerated grin popped up.

Gwyneth looked at Brian, who had slipped down so that his double chin was resting on his chest. His eyes were fixed on the Christmas tree lights. 'Be a while it will before he can play with that.'

'I know,' said Valerie. 'He's too young to understand. But next year'll be different. Me and Brian will take him to see Santa.'

'*Cau dy ceg.*'

'What?'

'It means shut your mouth. Always talking about your Brians you are. Next Christmas most of us won't see our babies so stop talking about it, will you now.'

Valerie swung round. 'Don't shout at me. It's not my fault you can't keep your baby. That you don't know who the father is.'

There was silence. All the girls looked at Gwyneth.

'Now look you here. I didn't say I didn't know, but my business it is, not yours.'

The angry vibes woke Eirlys who'd been asleep on her mother's knee. She began to cry and, one by one, the other babies joined in.

Miss M struggled to her feet. 'Right, mums. I think it best if you all take your babies to the nursery and settle them down before lunch.'

Paula sounded the dinner gong at precisely one o'clock. The girls took their places at the table and began to pull crackers, put on paper hats and read out the corny jokes. Christine, her cheeks bright red, sweat clinging to her forehead, struggled in with the turkey.

'Oh Christine. You're due in less than a week. You should have let one of the mums do that.'

'It's all right, Miss M, I can manage.' She set the carving dish down in front of Nurse Harding who was brandishing the carving knife against the sharpening steel.

'She insisted on bringing it in herself,' said one of the other Ladies in Waiting who'd followed her in with tureens of crisp, golden roast potatoes, smooth, creamy mash, glazed carrots and Brussels sprouts.

As she carved the turkey and placed a slice of breast and a portion of dark meat on each plate, Nurse Harding, not known for making positive comments, said, 'I must say you've done us proud, Christine.'

Miss M surveyed the feast on the table before them. 'Yes, this is a lovely spread. Well done.'

As all the girls joined in with their praise, Christine glowed with pride: her hazel eyes sparkled, the care-worn expression she wore most of the time, vanished beneath a radiant smile.

Everyone was surprised when Paula actually volunteered to help with the washing up.

'Do the dishes every Christmas at home.' She paused to push up the sleeves of her new polo-neck sweater. 'Me dad and three brothers don't get back from the pub till after closing time. Never had a Christmas dinner before half past three and by the time we're finished they're all half cut.'

Gwyneth looked at the clock. 'Mam and Dad will be on their way to Beaumaris to see my Nan by now. She will be asking why I'm not there.'

'Well a lorra things have changed since last Christmas,' said Paula. 'Didn't know then what was gonna happen.'

There were eleven visitors at *The House* that afternoon: one set of parents, one auntie, the other eight were all for Valerie: Brian, his mum, his four younger brothers, his gran and his grandad. From her armchair at the other end of the room, Gwyneth watched the adults cooing over the babies. She became increasingly irritated with Brian's younger brothers: they screeched their racing cars across the floor, or made a monotonous drone through pursed lips as they held aeroplanes aloft in their fingertips and raced around the room.

What Valerie had said still hurt. How could she think that she had slept around and didn't know who Eirlys's father was? How could she? They hadn't spoken to each other since. Gwyneth couldn't stand watching the happy family scene any longer. She stood up. 'I'm going for a walk.'

'I'll come with you,' said Paula

'Hey, before you go will you take a photo?' Valerie held out a camera. 'Of us all.'

Paula glanced at Gwyneth and rolled her eyes. 'Right give it here. Now ger yerselves together. You and Brian on the sofa with the baby. Gran, Grandad and Mam behind. You lads sit on the floor. Ready. Say cheese.'

As they pushed the squeaky-wheeled prams to the park, Paula said, 'You don't wanna let Valerie get to you. Sometimes she don't think what she's saying, yer know whar I mean.'

'Because she's going to get married, she thinks she's better than us.'

'Well at least she's gorra fellar.' Paula took a long draw on her ciggie.

'But who'd want to spend the rest of their life with Brian?'

Paula laughed. 'Yea. You're right there.'

They sat on a bench and both girls stared across the park to where a little girl wearing a pixie hood, scarf and mittens was riding her new tricycle. Her mum and dad were holding hands and walking a few paces behind. She kept stopping and turning around, calling to her parents to look at how well she could pedal. They shouted back to be careful, not to get in people's way.

'I've decided I'm not keeping Gina, yer know.'

'But you said …'

'That was when I thought Gino was coming back. But it's never gonna work, me looking after a baby on me own, thinking all the time of that rotten bastard married, living in a nice house, buying his wife new clothes, and me with nothin'.'

Gwyneth put her arm round Paula's shoulders and held her close, their heads touching.

'Miss M's taking me and Gina to the adoption agency as soon as they open after Christmas.'

As they squeaked back up Granby Hill an ambulance pulled out of the drive of *The House*.

'Who was it?' asked Paula when they got back inside.

'Christine. She started soon after you left.'

'Good job she waited till she'd made Christmas dinner. Couldn't have done it without her. Not with Miss M laid up. Who's gonna make tea?'

Everyone looked at Valerie.

'All right, all right I'll do it.' She looked over at Gwyneth. 'Will you give me a hand?'

Valerie hacked at the turkey. Gwyneth buttered the cut end of the loaf before cutting a slice; she held the loaf up on end and sawed horizontally with the bread-knife. Best way to get a nice thin slice and make it go further Mam had always said.

The two girls still weren't speaking as they assembled the sandwiches and put them on the table, along with the Christmas cake and the trifle Christine had made the day before.

As they laid out the plates and the cutlery, Valerie said, 'Oh this is stupid. We can't fall out now.'

'I thought we were friends, like. And there is you thinking I don't know who is Eirlys's father.'

'It's just you never talk about him.'

'What is there to say?'

Christine's baby was born on Christmas day just before midnight. It was a boy with dark skin and black curly hair. She christened him Le-Roy.

CHAPTER 9

"There goes my everything"
Engelbert Humperdinck 1967

Miss M's influenza kept her in bed for several days. When she began to recover, Nurse Harding suggested a tonic to build up her strength and a holiday to provide a change of air. So, on the Thursday after Christmas, Miss M went to visit relatives - relatives she'd never mentioned before - leaving Nurse Harding in charge.

Valerie's baby was now five weeks old and still no decision about their future had been made. There'd been no more visits from her mother since the day angry words had been exchanged from opposite ends of the settee, just daily phone calls: Valerie held the receiver away from her ear, pulled a face, shrugged her shoulders and answered in monosyllables. Then she'd make the excuse that baby Brian was crying and hang up. In the end she'd told the girls that if the phone rang for her to say she was out.

Then on Friday 30 December, the day after Miss M left, Mrs Johnson called at *The House*. She waited in the hall while Gwyneth went upstairs to tell her daughter she was there. Valerie refused to come down so eventually Nurse Harding invited her mother into the office.

Gwyneth went back up to tell Valerie who raced down the stairs and banged on the office door. 'I know you're in there. I know you're talking about me.'

Nurse Harding opened the door and smiled. 'Well, Valerie, why don't you come in and join us.'

Gwyneth hung about outside but couldn't hear anything

that was said behind the closed door.

When they all came out half an hour later Valerie didn't look quite so angry, neither did her mother. Nurse Harding was smiling.

'What happened?' asked Paula as Nurse Harding went to see Mrs Johnson off in her car.

'I don't have to give Brian away. I can stay here. I had to agree to go back to school. Nurse Harding is going to look after Brian.'

'That's not fair,' said Paula. 'She wouldn't do that for me. I've gorra leave by the end of the week.'

'But you've decided to have Gina adopted. You don't need to stay here.'

'Nina kept her baby, but she wasn't allowed to stay here,' said Gwyneth.

'But my Mum won't let me live in a bed-sit. It took Nurse Harding a long time to persuade her to let me stay here.'

'So, why'd she do that?'

'Says she's become very fond of little Brian.'

'What, that dried up old cow?'

'Ssh Paula, she'll hear you.' Gwyneth nodded towards the front door.

The girls watched as Mrs Johnson drove away. Nurse Harding came back up the steps, the fingers of her right-hand curled round and held close to her side.

'What are you staring at? Get back to your chores.' Nurse Harding went into the medical room and closed the door.

'Well I'll tell you somethin' for nothin'.' I wouldn't want her looking after my baby.' Paula turned and ran up the stairs.

'You alright, Paula?' Gwyneth pushed open the bedroom door. She peered through the crack and could just see her friend's back as she lay on the bed. 'Will I come in?'

When there was no reply Gwyneth stepped inside. Paula was curled up in the foetal position. Within the curve of her body lay baby Gina, her tiny hand clutching her mother's finger, her eyes fixed on her face, which was wet with tears, black mascara in rivulets down her cheeks.

'Paula, *bach*, you mustn't upset yourself, now. Remember, you told me to take no notice of Valerie.'

'It's nor about that.' Paula wiped her face, leaving black streaks on the candlewick bedspread. 'Nurse Harding told me this morning they'd found a family for our Gina.' She looked down at the little girl in a pink polka dot dress and the sobbing started again. 'She goes to them the day after tomorrow.'

Gina began to wail. Paula pulled her daughter towards her and held her close, the tears rolled down her face onto the baby's spiky black hair.

Gwyneth sat down on the bed and didn't know what to say. There was nothing to say anyway. As she knew only too well, nothing that anyone could say would make things any better.

Paula pushed herself up, swung her legs over the edge of the bed and carried Gina over to the window. 'I just don't know whar I want anymore. I'm just doing what I gorra do. What's best for Gina. Oh! I really need a ciggie.'

'Here.' Gwyneth held out her arms. 'Give me Gina. I won't tell Nurse Harding you're smoking upstairs.'

Paula lit her cigarette and blew smoke out through the open window. 'Life is crap really.'

***

'It's for the best,' said Nurse Harding when the time came for Paula to hand over her baby.

97

They were standing in the hallway, Paula's suitcase already packed and waiting. Through the open door the girls heard the crunch of tyres on the gravel come to a stop at the foot of the front steps.

'Taxi for Harding.'

'Ta ra, Gina,' whispered Paula, stroking her baby's head. As she lifted her hand the dark hair with a mind of its own sprang back into a single vertical quiff. 'I hope your new …' the word mam stuck in Paula's throat '… can do somethin' with that hair!'

Nurse Harding took a step towards Paula. 'I'll take Gina now. Don't worry. She'll be fine.'

Paula hesitated, took one last, long look at her baby's face before handing her over. Then she let her empty arms drop down at her side and didn't attempt to brush away the tears that rolled down her cheeks as Nurse Harding carried Gina out through the front door and down the steps.

Gwyneth put her arm round Paula's shoulders, trying to stop her friend from shaking as she watched the nurse get into the back seat with baby Gina in her arms.

'Well good luck with the new job, Paula,' Nurse Harding called out as the taxi driver closed the rear door.

'As if you care,' muttered Paula standing on tip-toe and craning her neck to try and see through the side window to where Gina was lying in Nurse Harding's lap.

The engine started, the taxi moved off, paused for a few seconds in the gateway, then disappeared down the hill.

'Don't cry. It's alright,' said Valerie.

'You mean it's alright for you,' Paula sobbed. 'You're not giving your baby away. You don't know nothin'.'

'I'll come with you to the bus stop,' said Gwyneth.

'No, you stay here with Eirlys.'

'She is in her pram already. You wait by there while I get her.'

'No, I gorra do this on my own.' Paula sniffed then wiped her eyes with the back of her hand. 'But later if you wanna come and see me you know where I am ... though I'll not be in that bed-sit for long. I'll be lookin' for somethin' better. Yer know war I mean.'

When Paula had gone, Gwyneth went straight into the garden, lifted Eirlys out of the pram and took her upstairs to her room. She stood by the window with the sleeping baby in her arms staring out at the leafless branches on the trees and the cold, grey winter sky.

First Susan, then Nina, now Paula. All the girls that Gwyneth had got to know well were leaving. There were the new Ladies in Waiting of course, but they stuck together as they shared the same experiences and faced the same problems. The mums would sit with them in the knitting circle around the television in the evening and relate horrendous tales of long painful labours and complain about the endless sleepless nights, but they didn't strike up friendships with the new arrivals; they hadn't long left at *The House* and there just wasn't time. Valerie was the only one who had been around as long as Gwyneth. At least Valerie would be there until Gwyneth left, now that it had been agreed she could stay on with her baby if she went back to school.

***

Term started on Tuesday 3 January. At eight o'clock in the morning Mrs Johnson's Rover was at the foot of the front steps of *The House*, its engine running. She'd come to collect Valerie and take her to school, to be sure that her daughter actually got there, she said. Gwyneth couldn't help feeling sorry for Valerie as she stood in the hallway wearing a gymslip and school blazer. With tears in her eyes, she kissed baby Brian's head and told him to be good; it would only be eight hours before she was back to look after him. There was the sound of a car horn; Nurse Harding told Valerie to dry her eyes, hurry up and not keep her mother waiting.

Baby Brian wasn't happy. He refused his ten o'clock feed: as soon as the teat brushed his lips, his head turned away, his face puckered and inflamed with fury. Gwyneth watched Nurse Harding get more and more impatient as she tried again and again to get him to take the bottle. Her heart went out to the distraught baby. When Eirlys was fed, changed and out in the garden for an airing, she offered to take over. Nurse Harding handed over the screaming baby and headed for the peace and quiet of the medical room.

Gwyneth wrapped Brian in a blanket and held him close as she walked around the house and out into the garden to check on Eirlys, who was thankfully fast asleep. Eventually, hunger became more important than the comfort of Valerie's breast and the unhappy baby accepted the expressed milk from a bottle. He was asleep when the bell rang for lunch.

Eirlys woke up as the girls were still eating their rice pudding and, for once, Nurse Harding disregarded the rules and said Gwyneth could leave the table before everyone had finished. Rather than feeding her baby in the nursery, she could take Eirlys up to her bedroom, a practice not usually encouraged during the day. At the time, Gwyneth thought she was just showing her gratitude for the help she'd been with baby Brian that morning.

Who was that? Gwyneth looked down from the dormer window in her small attic room. The car parked in the driveway was familiar. A Rover. Gwyneth was sure that Mrs Johnson had said that Valerie would have to come back on the bus; she wasn't getting a lift home as well. Anyway, it was only two o'clock: school didn't end till three-thirty.

Eirlys had fallen asleep with her head resting on Gwyneth's shoulder, so she laid her gently in the cot and went back to the window to try and make out who was behind the wheel. Whoever it was didn't get out, just leaned across to open the passenger door. Someone came out of the house and walked round in front of the car, a woman wearing a white cap. Nurse Harding. She was carrying a baby wrapped in a blue blanket! Gwyneth suddenly felt very cold. They couldn't be. They wouldn't, would they? There must be some other explanation. Perhaps baby Brian was ill and they were taking him to the doctor. Maybe that was why he had been so distressed this morning. She had to find out what was going on, so she ran out onto the landing and down the two flights of stairs.

The front door had already closed when Gwyneth arrived in the hall. She pulled it open just in time to see the Rover pulling out of the drive, so she ran out onto the road waving her arms, but it was no use: the car was already out of sight.

'What's the matter?' asked a girl who'd only been at *The House* for a couple of days.

'Nurse Harding. Where's she gone?'

'Didn't say. Just that she'd be back around five.'

'Five! Valerie will be home from school at four. She'll go mental.'

***

The doorbell jangled continuously as the caller kept tugging on the bell-pull. Gwyneth hoped it was Nurse Harding bringing baby Brian back, but it wasn't. It was Valerie who dropped her satchel just inside the door and dashed down the hall. Gwyneth ran after her and stopped in the nursery doorway as Valerie looked down into the empty cot and screamed, 'Where is he? Where's Brian?'

'Nurse Harding took him out in the car.'

'What? Where did she take him?'

'I don't know.'

'Is he hurt? Is he ill?'

'I don't think so.'

'But he's due for a feed.'

'One of the girls says she took a bottle with her.'

'Why would she do that? I said I'd feed him when I got back.'

Gwyneth noticed the two wet patches on Valerie's school blouse.

'They've taken him away, haven't they?'

'We don't know that, mind.'

'They have. You should have stopped them.'

'Upstairs I was. When I got down by here …'

'You're my friend. You should have been there.' Valerie shrieked. 'It's all your fault.'

'But what was I to do?'

'I've got to find him …' Valerie ran out of the nursery and down the hall. '… before it's too late.'

Gwyneth caught up with her at the front door. 'So where is it you're going to look for him?'

'The adoption agency. You've been there. You know where it is. You can show me.'

'Miles away it is. By the time we get there it will be closed.'

Valerie leant her back against the wall. With a long drawn

out howl, she slowly slid down the wood panelling and crumpled into a heap on the floor.

Gwyneth crouched down beside her. 'You don't know that's where they've taken him.'

'You don't know my parents,' sobbed Valerie.

Nothing Gwyneth could say made any difference, so in the end she just sat there on the floor beside her distraught friend.

When they heard a car on the drive, they looked at each other and Valerie leapt to her feet. 'That'll be Nurse Harding back with Brian.' She threw open the door.

It was Nurse Harding but she wasn't carrying a baby. With her was Mrs Johnson and a man in a pin-stripe suit.

'Where's Brian?' Valerie yelled as she ran towards them. 'What have you done with him?' She beat her fists against Nurse Harding's chest.

The man grabbed Valerie's arms and pinned them behind her back.

Nurse Harding took a deep breath and brushed down the front of her uniform. 'I think we'd all better go into the office.'

'Leave me alone, Dad.' Valerie kicked out at the shins of the man who was dragging her in through the door into Miss M's office.

Mrs Johnson slammed the door shut and the other girls, who had come down to see what all the commotion was about, looked at each other. Gwyneth couldn't bear to listen to Valerie's screams so she fetched Eirlys from her cot in the nursery and took her upstairs.

At teatime Nurse Harding told the girls that Valerie wouldn't be joining them as she was resting in sickbay and would be sleeping there overnight.

'But what's the matter with her?' asked Christine.

'Overtired,' said Nurse Harding. 'You know what it's like when you've just had a baby. Emotions all over the place.'

'But she was fine yesterday.'

Nurse Harding gave a superior smile. 'Some girls try so hard to hide their feelings, but then all that bottled-up emotion has to come out sometime. They call it the Baby Blues.'

'But what about Brian?'

'Well, the doctor has said she's not to have any visitors.'

'Not her boyfriend. I mean the baby.'

'He's just fine and he's being looked after.'

'But where is he?'

'That I'm afraid I can't say.' Nurse Harding refused to be drawn any further.

***

'Where's Valerie?' Gwyneth asked the following morning at breakfast.

Nurse Harding looked round at all the girls at the table before she replied. 'Valerie's parents took her home late last night.'

'I thought I heard a car around about midnight,' said one of the new mums.

'Valerie won't be coming back.' Nurse Harding concentrated on buttering her toast.

'Her baby. Where is he?' asked Gwyneth.

'He's been taken into care and will be put up for adoption.'

'What?' Gwyneth exclaimed. 'Why?'

'Well, you all saw how Valerie behaved yesterday. How violent she was. We have to think of the baby's safety.'

'Violent! Only because you took her baby away.'

'She's only sixteen. Still a child. Not mature enough to care for a baby.'

'*Rwtsh lol*,' said Gwyneth. 'Knows more about babies does Valerie … than anyone else here.'

'That's enough.' said Nurse Harding. 'Social workers and doctors feel that it's in the best interests of the baby if he's adopted.'

'It do seem to me that no one is thinking about Valerie.'

Nurse Harding shrugged. 'She'll get over it.'

'I must talk with her.' Gwyneth realised she didn't know where Valerie lived. 'Will you give me her address or phone number, Nurse Harding?'

'No. Her parents made it quite clear that I wasn't to pass on any contact details. They think that keeping in touch with anyone from here will just make it much harder for Valerie to forget what has happened and put the past behind her.'

CHAPTER 10

"Green Green grass of home"
Tom Jones 1967

The front door opened and shut. Footsteps on the parquet floor echoed in the hallway. A familiar face appeared in the doorway.

'Miss M.' Nurse Harding half rose from the chair at the head of the table, her mouth set in a fixed smile, her eyes narrowed and wary. 'What a surprise. We were expecting you to be away for at least a fortnight.'

'Oh, after a week I felt so much better. Must be the sea air.'

'We were just finishing high tea. Do you want to sit here?'

'No, you stay where you are. I'll take your chair.' Miss M unpinned her turquoise hat, took off her coat, laid them on the settee and walked to the far end of the table.

Christine scooped a generous helping of pudding into a bowl and the girls passed it down to Miss M.

She looked at creamy yellow custard topped by fluffy white meringue. 'This looks delicious.'

'I made it myself,' said Christine. 'Queen of Puddings. Cook says it's a good way of using up stale bread and cake crumbs and you only need milk, eggs, a bit of sugar and jam so it doesn't cost much either.'

'Very good. And how's little Le-Roy?'

'Oh, he's lovely, Miss M.'

'And I see we have some new faces.'

Nurse Harding introduced the three girls sitting on her

left.

'Well, I'll have a little chat with each of you tomorrow. I hope you'll feel at home here with us for the next few months. We all try to help and care for each other. Don't we girls?' Miss M turned her attention to the other side of the table. 'Paula's gone, I see.'

'Yes,' said Gwyneth. 'Living in Fulham she is now and working at Harrods.'

'And little Gina went for adoption.' Miss M nodded her head. 'But where's Valerie? I thought she'd still be here.'

'She's gone,' said Gwyneth. 'So quick it was. No time to say goodbye.'

Miss M frowned and stared down the length of the table. 'But where's she gone, Nurse Harding?'

'Back home. Back to school.'

'And the baby?'

The girls sat, silent as spectators at a Wimbledon final, following the bad vibrations bouncing back and forth along the length of the dining-room table.

'He's being adopted.'

'What! Valerie would never agree to that.'

'I'll tell you about that later this evening, Muriel.'

Even the girls washing up in the kitchen at the back of the house could hear the raised voices behind the closed office door. Then on her way upstairs to check on the babies, Gwyneth saw Nurse Harding come out and cross the hall to the medical room, her eyes blazing, her lips pinched together into a thin line. Miss M did not emerge from the office until after all the girls had gone to bed.

At breakfast the following morning, Miss M resumed her position at the head of the table.

'Do you know is Valerie alright, Miss M?' asked

Gwyneth. 'Nurse Harding wouldn't say.'

'I rang her parents' house last night, but they said she couldn't come to the phone.'

'Will you give me her address?'

'Her mother specifically said no further contact.'

'There is a pity. Going to write to her I was.'

'I'm sorry.' Miss M stood up. 'Now let's say grace. We won't wait for Nurse Harding. She won't be down for breakfast this morning.'

In fact, Nurse Harding never did appear for breakfast again. However, she did take her place at lunch and high tea, but rarely joined in the conversation and always avoided eye contact with Miss M. A few days later she announced that she had decided to resume her travels around Europe: a couple of weeks in Paris then on down to Rome.

How odd. Gwyneth was sure she remembered Nurse Harding saying that she was planning to stay at *The House* until summer to save up for the trip. Then across Gwyneth's mind flashed a scene that had borne no significance at the time: Mrs Johnson's car driving off. Nurse Harding's clenched fist held close to her side as she hurried back up the steps, across the hall into the medical room and closed the door.

***

Gwyneth was in the nursery, bathing her baby for the last time. She lifted Eirlys out of the water and cocooned her in a towel. 'There's a nice clean babby you are.'

As she patted her dry, paying particular attention to the folds of skin under the arms and at the top of her legs, Gwyneth couldn't believe how much she had grown. Six pounds six ounces at birth and now six weeks later she was eight and a half pounds.

Christine came into the nursery and greeted Gwyneth with a smile. Most of the girls couldn't wait until their time hiding from the world was over, but not Christine. Since her culinary success at Christmas, her smile had triumphed over her cowed expression, her hazel eyes sparkled, especially when she was with baby Le-Roy.

She laid her baby down on a changing mat and began pulling apart the poppers on his sleep-suit. 'You're leaving tomorrow, aren't you?'

'Yes.' Gwyneth sprinkled talcum powder over Eirlys's bottom.

'And what's happening to your baby?'

'Being adopted, she is.'

'I don't want my Le-Roy to be adopted, but Miss M says it's very hard looking after a baby all on your own.'

Gwyneth glanced over at little Le-Roy with his tightly curled hair, his coffee-coloured skin. From what Christine had said about the father while she was expecting, many of the girls had suspected that her baby would be of mixed race. They had tutted and gossiped. When Christine brought Le-Roy back to *The House* their prejudice had melted away and they cooed over him saying 'how sweet'. But behind Christine's back they said that no one would want to adopt him. He'd have to go into Barnardo's or be fostered.

'I can't take him home,' said Christine. 'Not with Mam always drinking. And how will I get the money to look after him? I'm not clever enough to get a job.'

'Don't say that. You it was who cooked Christmas dinner.'

'But that's different. You don't have to read to do that.'

Gwyneth couldn't help wondering if in the end the decision about whether or not to keep her baby would be taken out of Christine's hands, just like what had happened to Valerie.

***

Gwyneth had now sat in all the eighteen chairs around the dining-room table. She'd moved down one side as her pregnancy progressed, overtaken Nurse Harding at the far end then continued up the home straight as her baby grew older. Now she was sitting on Miss M's right-hand side. She would be the next one to leave.

'You're sure, are you? Sure, you want to go ahead with the adoption?' asked Miss M.

Gwyneth nodded.

'If there's a chance you'll change your mind it's best to do it now. You don't sign the final papers giving up all rights until your baby is six months old. But after today it will be difficult getting her back and very upsetting for the adoptive parents.'

'I will not change my mind.'

'Very well, then. Monday morning eleven o'clock.'

Gwyneth had watched too many girls cry when they gave their babies away; she'd seen too many sad farewells on the steps of *The House*. It wasn't going to be like that for her and Eirlys.

If she left promptly at eleven that would allow enough time to walk to the Tube station, and for the journey up the Northern line to catch the twelve-thirty train. After breakfast, Eirlys in her bouncy chair looked on while Gwyneth made up the bottles that someone else would give her. She just sat there her eyes fixed on her mother, didn't cry; it was as if she knew.

If only. If only there was some other way. But Gwyneth been through all this so many times before. Take Eirlys home? No chance. She could see her mother's face, hear her father's words: "Brought shame to our door, you have". Though how he could say that after what he'd done. If it wasn't for him, she wouldn't be here making the decision that would break her heart. If he hadn't committed adultery then Geraint would never have been born, she wouldn't have fallen in love with him and he wouldn't have been able to father Eirlys. Poor Eirlys. None of this was her fault. She didn't deserve a grandmother who thought she was conceived in sin, a grandfather, twice over, who'd call her a bastard.

If she couldn't take her home, she could stay in London, look for work. But what was she qualified to do? Look at Paula: if anyone could talk her way into a job, find a landlord willing to rent to an unmarried mother, Paula could. But even Paula had given up. Nina had managed to keep her baby, but she was willing to scrub floors, wash dishes, look after other people's children. Gwyneth wanted more out of life. Keeping Eirlys would mean she could never train as a teacher. Her baby deserved a mother who was desperate for a child to love, not someone who would always hanker after a career she'd been forced to give up.

Gwyneth bent down and lifted Eirlys out of her chair. With a hand clasped around each side of the tiny chest she held her at arms-length. 'There is nothing else to be done. I don't want to, but I have to do this. If I keep you there are tongues in plenty to tittle-tattle and fingers to point. Please, *Cariad*, when you are older, please understand I did this for you and don't think bad of me.'

Upstairs in her bedroom, Gwyneth laid Eirlys on the bed and took off her clothes. She folded a clean terry-towelling square with care; it would be her baby's new mother who would take it off. As she lifted the tiny legs to put the baby's nappy in place, she marvelled again at how they'd grown from thin and bony to so chubby that they now creased at the ankles and knees. She fastened the safety pin, then bent down, put her lips against Eirlys's tummy and blew a raspberry. This had been part of the nappy-changing routine for a few weeks now. Even though her baby still couldn't smile, Gwyneth was sure that the way she stretched out her legs and wiggled her toes meant that Eirlys enjoyed the feel of a rush of warm breath on her skin.

Gwyneth stretched the neck of the vest with two hands then held the front edge under Eirlys's chin while she gently eased the back over her head. How frightened she'd been the first time her fingers had felt the soft depression on top of Eirlys's head. The nurse had come over and asked whatever was the matter, then explained all babies were like that: it was called the fontanelle. Gwyneth peered closely at Eirlys's scalp; all traces of the yellow, scaly layer were gone. She had thought it was her fault for not caring for her baby properly, until Miss M had said it was only cradle-cap and given her a bottle of special shampoo.

It had been hard to decide on a going-away outfit for Eirlys. At first Gwyneth had chosen a pink gingham dress with a lace trim on the puff sleeves and the hem, but then decided it wouldn't be warm enough for January. She couldn't have the new parents thinking that she was an irresponsible mother so she had searched through the bookshelves in the nursery and selected a pram suit instead. As she eased the tiny arms into the soft woollen sleeves of the matinee coat and slid the leggings up over the baby's dimpled knees, Gwyneth felt a pang of guilt; she hadn't knitted even a pair of booties or a bonnet as a keepsake for

Eirlys to take to her new home. But she told herself it didn't matter: her baby was leaving her past behind, starting again with a new family, a new name. Gwyneth hoped that no one would ever tell Eirlys she was adopted so she'd never want to find her real parents. It was better that way.

Quarter to eleven. Fifteen minutes, that's all they had left and then they'd be parted forever. Someone else would care for her baby for the next two decades: they'd watch her first tottering steps, they'd be waiting at the gates after her first day at school, they'd see her grow into a young woman and hopefully they wouldn't do what Gwyneth's own mother had done and desert her when a love affair ended in tears.

The tears that Gwyneth had been struggling to control were shed in those last ten minutes with Eirlys in the small attic room. Then she blew her nose, dried her eyes, picked up her baby and took her downstairs. Miss M was waiting.

'I'll always be thinking about you, *Cariad*,' Gwyneth whispered as she kissed the top of Eirlys's head. The light covering of down against her lips felt like the skin of a fresh peach. She inhaled the smell of Johnson's baby powder and partially digested milk.

***

It was over a mile to the Tube station. The suitcase was heavy, but Gwyneth didn't take the bus. She needed the time to make the transition from mother back to teenager. Although it was a relief to be responsible just for herself, not to have to constantly consider the needs of another human being, there was also an emptiness, a loss, a feeling of guilt, of having failed, of having given up.

The Tube rattled its way northward, everyone in the carriage insulated in their own private world, their own problems. Perhaps she should have let Miss M take a photograph of Eirlys; she hadn't in case someone at home found it and asked who it was. She would always remember what her baby looked like. Gwyneth closed her eyes and mentally explored her baby's face: the chubby cheeks, the snub nose, she could see the tiny rosebud mouth moving and hear the little grunting noise she made in her sleep, but she couldn't quite remember the subtle shades of her baby's skin. She tried to memorise every detail, but the image was blurring, the smell of Johnson's powder and baby milk was fading.

She panicked. There was still time to change her mind.

She must go back, fetch her daughter before she forgot what she looked like.

Gwyneth got up and stood holding her suitcase behind a young couple with a small child waiting near the sliding doors. She would get off at the next station, cross to the other platform and get the southbound train. Before they reached the next station, the train slowed then came to a halt. The little girl began to whimper and held her hands up to her mother who scooped her up. When the train remained stationary in the dark tunnel, the child became even more anxious and cried even louder. Her father played peek-a-boo from behind his newspaper and by the time they moved off there was a smile on the tear-stained face. Maybe it was seeing a proper family with two parents, maybe it was realising that Eirlys would now be well on the way to her new home: Gwyneth would never really know which but she put her case down on the floor and went back to her seat and tried, without success, to hold back the tears. When they noticed her crying, the other passengers looked away. Only the woman sitting opposite seemed concerned: she bent forward as if about to say something, then must have thought better of it, for she leant back in her seat and she too turned away.

***

Her case was already up on the rack and she'd settled herself down in a window seat on the London to Holyhead express before Gwyneth realised that she was in a smoking compartment. Too exhausted to move after a day of tears on top of more than a month of disturbed nights, she fell asleep. When she woke the train was pulling out of Crewe. The young lad opposite smiled and offered her a cigarette.

'There is kind of you, but I don't smoke.' Gwyneth shook her head remembering the ciggie Paula had given her, how she couldn't stop coughing. How was Paula? Was she still at Harrods? Had she managed to find a better flat?

The lad wasn't about to give up. 'From Wales, are you?'
She nodded.
'Going home, then?'
'Yes, to Anglesey. Llangefni.'
'Been working in London, have you?'
'Looking after my aunt. She's not been well.'
'So, she's better now, is she?'
'Much better.'
'So, what will you do when you get home?'
'Help on the farm. Maybe get a little job, earn some money for when I go to college.'
'You going to college, then?'
'I was supposed to start teacher training at Bangor last year but my aunt was ill, see.'

The small talk continued, Gwyneth on her guard not to let anything slip, struggling to convince herself that the lie she would have to tell everyone back home was true.

The lad got off at Chester. Gwyneth took out the diary

116

she'd been given as a Christmas present. She opened it at the week beginning Monday 8 January 1967 – then flicked over the pages: another seven months until September when she could leave home again. She'd mark time until then. Tell no one about Eirlys, not even Geraint. Before putting the diary away, she turned to the inside of the front cover and there in Miss M's copperplate handwriting were the words:

Today is the first day of the rest of your life.

PART 2

Gwyneth & Eirlys

Valerie & Brian

Susan & Chloe

Paula & Gina

Nina & baby

Christine & Le-Roy

CHAPTER 11

"Take a look at me now"
Phil Collins 1984

The words "You're no child of mine" had punctuated Anna's childhood. Uttered by her father whenever she misbehaved: made too much noise, too much mess, spoke with her mouth full or answered back, anything in fact that disrupted his ordered life, these words came to mean that she wasn't the little girl he wanted her to be, hadn't achieved what was expected of her. In fact, as far as he was concerned, she could never do anything right. In the end she'd stopped trying and now her spiky hair was dyed purple and her eyes framed with thick black lines. This had rendered him speechless and he had resorted to condemning her with a silent, piercing stare, a long drawn out sucking-in of breath, then marching from the room and slamming the door.

Then when she was eighteen, she learnt the cruel truth of her father's words.

It was the day after her "coming of age" birthday that her Dad left home and went to live with his mistress. Looking back from a more grown-up perspective, Anna wondered why her parents hadn't split up before: after all they'd led separate lives, slept in separate beds. There'd been angry silences for as long as she could remember. Perhaps, like other couples whose marriages had gone sour, they were just staying together for the sake of the children or in their case their only child.

Anna didn't miss him. Her mum, however, was devastated. She retired to her bed while dust and disorder descended on the house she'd always kept spotless. When the minister came around to find out why she wasn't at church, he summoned the doctor who prescribed happy pills to help her through this difficult time.

It was a couple of weeks later, after another pastoral visit, that her mum had come to sit beside Anna on the sofa. 'There's something I must tell you.'

Anna moved her hand away from her mouth, curled her fingers into her palm and examined her bitten nails. 'If it's about Dad, I don't want to know.'

'No, it's about you.'

'Me?'

'Reverend Clegg says we should have told before.'

'Told me what?'

Her mum stared down at the rose-patterned carpet. 'It was me you see, me who didn't want to tell you. Wanted to believe you were mine.'

'I was yours? What d'you mean?'

'That I'd given birth to you.'

'What?'

'You came to us when you were six weeks old.'

'You mean …' Anna leant back and clasped her arms around her chest. 'You mean...'

Her mum nodded. 'We adopted you.'

'How could you?' Anna stood up, walked over to the window and gazed out at the frost-covered lawn. 'How could you not tell me?'

'I'm sorry, but I needed you to love me. I thought if you knew I wasn't your real mother you wouldn't.'

Anna couldn't get her head round the fact that the woman she had always called Mum wasn't her real mother. Then she recalled how the other children had mistaken the white-haired woman waiting at the school gates for her grandmother, and wondered why she had never suspected before.

The fact that her dad wasn't her dad didn't matter. It all made sense now. He hadn't wanted her, just gone along with the adoption to please her mother, then felt trapped for the next eighteen years, reluctantly honouring the commitment he'd made, then getting out the moment it was over.

There was some consolation in the fact that the couple she had always known as her parents weren't her real family. She didn't belong to them. When her father had kept telling her she was turning out just like her mother, he hadn't meant that she was becoming a timid woman whose horizons didn't stretch any further than the housework and the Mother's Union; he meant she was acting like her real mother.

But what was her real mother like? The anger bubbled up inside her. How could her real mother have just given her away? How could she forget all about her? Didn't she even wonder how her daughter was getting on, what she looked like, if she was happy?

Then came the daydreaming. Her real mother was famous. She hadn't wanted to give up her baby, but for the sake of her career she had to. Her real mother was a film star, a pop singer. Anna listed all the female celebrities she knew who were in their late thirties or early forties. She'd probably seen her mother on the screen. Of course, she remembered the baby she'd given birth to, but she couldn't admit to having a love child, couldn't risk losing the adoration of her fans, or her next contract. But that made her sound heartless, didn't it?

What about her real father? Maybe he didn't even know

she existed; his former lover hadn't told him she was pregnant. But then, perhaps she was just the result of a one-night stand; her mother didn't even know who her father was. No, no she didn't want to think about that. She wanted to be the result of a love affair that was thwarted, that could never continue. Her parents were both married to someone else: her father not able to leave his ailing wife, her mother forced to give her up, when her husband found out she was carrying another man's child.

It was several weeks before idle daydreaming gave way to reality. More likely her mother was a woman who had more children than she could manage or just a teenager who knew nothing of contraception. But whatever the circumstances, of her birth, she needed to know, so she could fill in the gaps, join up the dots and move on with her life.

'Mum, I'd like to find out about my real mother.'

'Real! Real? What does that make me?'

'Natural mother, then … birth mother. I need to find her.'

'Why?'

'So I know who I am, where I come from.'

'I wish I'd never told you.'

'Why did you then?'

'I thought it would make you feel better knowing that the man who's left us wasn't your father.'

'Will you help me then … to find my birth mother?'

'They told us at the agency that it was best for everyone if there was no contact at all. Ever.'

'Best for who? You? They never thought about those babies they were giving away. Did they? Never thought how we'd feel when we grew up.'

***

Anna climbed to the top deck of the bus, took a seat right at the back and opened a packet of Players. That was the only good thing about her job on the production line at the tobacco factory: free fags. And why did she have such a dead-end job? It was all her dad's fault. Before she left school, he'd made it quite clear that there was no way he was going to put any child of his through drama school. But she wasn't his child anyway; she no longer called him Dad. On the odd occasion he was mentioned she referred to him as Mr Harris.

She struck a match and watched as the tip of the cigarette glowed bright red then, with a flick of the wrist, extinguished the match and dropped it on the floor. What state would Brenda be in when she got home tonight? Since she'd found out the truth, Anna couldn't bring herself to call her adoptive mother Mum so used her first name, Brenda, instead.

She let herself in the front door expecting to find Brenda lying on the sofa, spaced out on the happy pills. But she wasn't. The smell of fried onions wafted down the hall.

'Shepherd's pie. Your favourite.' Brenda came out of the kitchen carrying a casserole dish which she took through to the dining room and placed on a mat on the already-laid table. 'What are you staring at? Come and sit down.'

Anna did as she was told.

When she'd dished out two generous helpings, Brenda said, 'I've been thinking, perhaps, there's still time for you to apply for drama school.'

'What?'

'Well, he can't stop you anymore. Now that he's gone, you'll be entitled to a grant. You still have the forms, don't you?'

That evening they filled in the application form: listed Anna's ballet and music certificates, the plays she'd been in at school, the amateur dramatic society she belonged to. It was past the closing date but they sent it in anyway, expecting to hear nothing and to have to repeat the process all over again later in the year.

Anna decided not to push her luck and left asking Brenda about her birth mother for another time. No point in risking more tears. The thoughts, however, continued to whirl round in her head: Where did she come from? What were her real parents like? Why had they given her away? What would her life have been like if they'd kept her? It had to be better than what it was: an only child brought in to save an empty marriage. Then she could stand it no longer.

'Brenda, please, I have to know.'

The birth certificate was no help: it was a short one and gave just her name and date of birth. At the bottom were the words: "compiled from the records of the Registrar General on 1st May 1967".

'That was when we officially adopted you,' said Brenda.

'So, you've no idea where I came from?'

'Well you must have been born in South London, fairly near where we lived at the time.' Brenda pointed to the certificate. 'Because the registration district is Lambeth. And yes, I'd almost forgotten. Your father …' She stopped and bit her lip. 'I mean …'

'It's OK. You mean Mr Harris.'

'Well anyway he said I must be mistaken, must be imagining things, but I was sure it was her.'

'Who?'

'The woman who handed you over at the adoption

agency, I saw her one day, before we moved up here. I followed her up Granby Hill and watched her go into a large Victorian house. Number 13.'

'Who was she?'

'I thought she might be your grandmother.'

CHAPTER 12

"Missing You"
Diana Ross 1985

Anna studied the A to Z; there was a Tube station not too far from Granby Hill. So far, finding her way had been easy. She'd arrived at the drama school in plenty of time so she could do her warm-up routine before the audition. Yes, the audition! She still couldn't believe it. They'd been so late in submitting the application form she hadn't even expected a reply, but here she was in London.

Now it was over. It hadn't been as bad as she'd imagined: she'd rehearsed her pieces so well she could have performed them anywhere, even the singing had been OK. But would they offer her a place? Who knows? When she'd left half an hour ago they'd just said that they'd be in touch.'

'Come home as soon as it's finished,' Brenda had said. Anna traced the route on the underground map. It was quite straightforward: instead of going north to St Pancras on the northern line, she could go south instead. 'Now be sure not to miss the six o'clock train,' Brenda had warned. It was only two fifteen. That gave her almost four hours to go and look for Granby Hill. Not that she thought for a minute that her real mother still lived there, if, indeed, she ever had. But there was a small chance that someone there would know something about the previous occupants. Anyway, she couldn't go home to Nottingham without at least trying to find out something about her history. After all, how do you know where you're going in life if you don't know where you've come from?

Just inside the ticket barrier was a blackboard. The chalked message read: *Body on the line. Anyone, who witnessed this incident on 22nd Jan 1985 please contact London Transport Police.* An icy draught whistled up the escalator. Anna shivered. For all she knew her birth mother could be dead.

The Tube hurtled through tunnels. None of the passengers spoke. Engrossed in their own private worlds, they stared at the adverts for holidays and headache tablets. Her birth mother could be here. They could have passed on the street, sat together on a bus; neither of them would have known.

Anna emerged from the underground. Directly opposite was a bingo hall, the new neon lights not quite concealing shadows of the original name, *Majestic,* outlined above the foyer of this old cinema. It was raining so she put her head down and battled her way past a parade of shops, then row upon row of identical terraced houses until she reached Granby Hill. She started up the steep climb: 7, 9, 11. The one with the *FOR SALE* board in the front garden must be number 13. It was a large, three-storey, detached house: slates teetered on the edge of the roof; water gushed from a fractured drain pipe. The remnants of what had once been gates hung, warped and rotten, from rusty hinges on the two pairs of gate posts. Anna walked up the semi-circular drive and climbed the six chipped, stone steps where weeds thrived in the cracks. There was no knocker, only a long, wrought-iron handle on the wall beside the door. She hesitated, before giving it a pull. Her guess had been right; a bell jangled deep within. The loud noise deterred her from pulling it again. She waited. After what seemed like an age, Anna thought she heard a faint shuffling inside.

The door was opened by a woman, probably in her late

seventies. Frizzy grey hair sprouted from her head; she wore a thick cardigan and stout lace-up shoes.

She peered through the thick lenses in plastic frames held together with sellotape. 'Yes.'

The words Anna had rehearsed flew from her head.

'Can I help you?'

'I ... I don't know. I'm looking for someone.'

'What's her name?'

Her name. Anna stared at the stooped figure in the doorway and wondered how this old lady knew that it was a woman, not a man, she was looking for.

'Is she a relative?'

'I think my mother might once have lived here.'

A smile broke out on the wrinkled face and the old lady opened the door wide. 'You'd better come in, dear.'

As Anna stepped into the hall, leaving footprints in the dust on the parquet floor, the smell of rising damp and mothballs came to greet her. Dust-coated cobwebs hung between the ceiling cornice and the picture rail.

'I thought that's why you'd come, dear, but I couldn't ask you outright. You see, I made that mistake a couple of years ago. The young lady looked quite taken aback. She'd only come to ask me what brand of washing powder and baked beans I bought.'

Anna hesitated.

'Oh, sorry I'm rambling on. Come into the office.' The old lady opened a door on the left. 'My, you are wet. Didn't you bring a coat?'

Brenda's last words as they stood on the platform that morning had been 'Where's your coat? You'll catch your death,' but Anna hadn't taken any notice, just boarded the train wearing her new black, bat-winged sweater and leggings: a most unsuitable outfit for an interview, her adoptive mother had said.

'Come and sit down by the fire.' The old lady patted the cushions on one of the two sagging armchairs and bent down to switch the gas fire from miser rate to medium. Then she picked up a crumpled paper bag from the hearth. 'Have a pear drop, dear.'

Anna accepted the sticky sweet.

'First you can tell me all about it. Then we'll make a pot of tea.'

All the thoughts that Anna had kept to herself, poured out. The old lady only made the odd sympathetic grunt or gesture and leant forward, nodding and sucking her sweet.

When Anna finished, she handed her a tissue and murmured, 'You do know what this house used to be?'

'No.'

'Oh, don't look so scared, dear. It was only a Mother and Baby Home. It was called *The House of Help*.'

'*The House of Help*!'

'Yes, girls used to come here when they were in trouble. They stayed until six weeks after the baby was born.'

'And then where did they go?'

'Those who put their babies up for adoption usually went back home. They often explained their absence as looking after a sick relative or working away. Though I was never sure that was wise.'

'So, you might know where my mother went.' Anna looked down at her hands. The tissue lay shredded in her lap.

'I can see how important it is to you, dear.' The old lady paused then continued, 'Have you thought what you'd do if you found her?'

'I'd write her a letter.'

'How would you feel if she didn't reply?'

'I'd be disappointed, but she'd probably have reasons. At least I'd have tried.'

Holding onto the arm of the chair to steady herself, the old lady heaved herself up. 'Now let's make that tea.' She paused with her hand on the door-knob. Anna realised she was expected to follow.

Only one bulb illuminated the wood-panelled hallway, so neither of them saw him until he had reached the bottom of the stairs.

'Oh Le-Roy, you did make me jump.'

'Sorry.' A lad about Anna's age grinned. 'I didn't mean to give you a fright.'

'Never mind. We're just going to have some tea. Would you like to join us?'

Anna felt Le-Roy's remarkable hazel eyes peruse her as he hesitated.

'Got to go. Don't want to be late for my shift.'

'How's your mum?'

'OK.' He looked back up the stairs. 'She's sleeping now.'

As the front door closed behind him the old lady said, 'Le-Roy's a grand lad, looks after his mum … works on the underground.'

On their way down the passage to the back of the house she bent down to rub her knee. 'Arthritis, you know. Can't get about as I used to.'

Through a door to her left Anna caught a glimpse of a room lined with shelves, floor-to-ceiling.

'A library but no books.' The old lady smiled. 'We used it as the nursery. Have a look inside, if you like.'

'So, I must have been in here as a baby?'

Just inside the door, next to a stack of yellow and green plastic buckets, a white, oval-shaped bath, decorated with a faded duck motif, balanced on a wooden stand. Half a dozen assorted babies' bottles gathered dust on one of the bookshelves, but the rest of the shelves were empty. On the floor beneath them, wooden frames, the canvas slings tacked to the top bars frayed and hanging loose, were folded and stacked, like sun-bleached, miniature deckchairs abandoned on the beach.

The old lady followed Anna into the library-cum-nursery. 'Not much left now, apart from the cots. When we closed down at the end of 1983, we told the last few girls they could take anything they needed.'

'Why did you close?'

'Times change, dear. When we opened my girls were called unmarried mothers, their babies illegitimate. Today it's one-parent families and love-children. Society is a lot more tolerant these days. Although I'm not sure it hasn't gone that little bit too far. Now let's go and make that tea.'

The kitchen was high-ceilinged with ancient appliances lining the walls. In the centre stood a sturdy table, its wooden surface worn smooth with generations of scrubbing. The old lady only partly filled the catering-size kettle then struck a match and lit the gas on the cast-iron cooker.

'So, was it just you and the girls who lived here?'

'We were supposed to have a resident nurse, but they were never resident very long. Said the pay was too low, the house too draughty, they never met anyone from the outside world. But we did have some visitors, you know. The girls used to entertain their friends, families or sometimes boyfriends over there in the sitting room across the way.'

Anna helped make the tea, with tea-leaves from a tea-caddy. 'Where's the milk kept?' she hesitated. 'I'm sorry, I don't know your name.'

'In there.' The old lady indicated a fridge towering in the corner. 'My girls always called me Miss M. You can call me that if you like.'

Miss M rummaged in the cupboard and brought out a packet of chocolate biscuits. 'I keep these for my visitors.'

Anna carried the tray laid with teapot, milk jug and sugar bowl, chipped china cups and a plate of biscuits, through to the office. As she pushed the door open and backed into the room, a voice inside cried, 'Who's that? Who's there?' She almost dropped the tray.

Miss M laughed. 'It's all right, dear. It's only Percival, the budgie. Le-Roy bought him for me when the last girl left. Said I needed someone else as well as him and his mum to talk to.'

'To talk to. To talk to.'

'Quiet now, Percy. Just put the tray down there, dear.' Miss M indicated a space on the hearth between the two armchairs. 'My girls weren't bad girls you know. Very few wanted to give up their babies. There were tears and heartache. They just did what they thought was best, or sometimes what others thought best.'

'So, will you be able to help me find my mother?'

'How old are you, dear?'

'Eighteen.'

Miss M nodded. 'So, you are old enough to apply for a copy of your original birth certificate, but before you get it you must have a counselling session with a social worker.'

'Why?'

'It's the law. The 1976 Adoption Act. But that's much

better than it was before: then there was no way adopted children could find out who their parents were.'

Anna poured the tea.

The old lady continued, 'When the law changed someone from the adoption agency came to see me, explained it all. I said I could do the counselling, but she said no, I wasn't trained. Not trained! I've been here since the place opened, listened to my girls while they sorted out what to do. But we didn't call it counselling back then, nor did we expect to get paid for it!'

Miss M offered Anna a biscuit and took a sip of tea before going on. 'In the end we agreed, if anyone came here looking for their mother then I'd give them the agency's phone number and they'd take over. The social worker said she'd be back for the girls' record cards.' She indicated a long, green metal box on a table next to the roll-top desk. 'But she hasn't, not in all these nine years. Said they wanted to put them on something that sounded like a microwave.'

'Microfiche.' suggested Anna.

'Yes, perhaps that's what she said.'

Anna's eyes were now scanning a huge notice-board. Pinned to it were photographs of babies, at least a hundred, possibly more: babies in prams, babies in cots, babies in baths; babies on their mother's knee, none of them more than a few weeks old. She realised then that the first photo she'd seen of herself had been taken in 1967 even though her birthday was at the end of 1966. 'Is one of those pictures of me?'

'Probably. I took one of all the babies before they left.'

'And these?' Anna pointed to one corner where the children were older, some in school uniform.

'Some of my girls still write, send me Christmas cards.'

'So, some of them did keep their babies.'

'Only a few. Most of those photos are of the children they've had since they left.'

'What about my birth mother, does she still write?'

'I'm sorry, dear, but, as I said, even if I did know who your mum was, I can't tell you, not until you've had counselling and realise how finding her might affect not only you but other people too. You see, back then mothers were told their babies would not be able to find them. Their secret was safe. We told the adopting families that the children would never be able to discover their original names or find their parents. I thought at the time it was all wrong.'

'But Brenda, I mean my adoptive mum, said she didn't mind if I found my real mother. She even told me that someone in this house might be able to help me find her.'

'Maybe she says that now, but if you did find your birth mother and decided to go and see her, she might feel you didn't want her anymore.'

'I'd only want to meet once to see what she's like, ask her why she gave me away.'

'But have you thought how your birth mother would feel if you suddenly turned up?'

'You mean she doesn't care about me? Doesn't wonder about me?'

'No, dear. But you see we had to warn the mums they would most likely never see their babies again, and encourage them to make a new life.'

'So, she'll have forgotten all about me?'

'Of course not. But things were different back then. Having a baby out of wedlock was frowned upon. If a girl hoped to get married, have a family in the future it was often best not to tell anyone about the child she'd had adopted.'

'So, you're telling me I shouldn't try to find my mother.'

Miss M leaned over and placed her hand over Anna's. 'I'm just trying to point out that it might not be as easy as you think.'

'But I just want to know who she was, why she gave me away. Couldn't you just look in there.' Anna inclined her head towards the green metal box.

'But it wouldn't help. Adoptive parents gave their babies new names.'

'But my birthday. They couldn't change that. It must be in there on my mother's record card.'

'I'm sorry. I wish I could help but I can't. You'll have to contact the adoption agency. They'll arrange the counselling and help you to apply for a copy of your birth certificate.' Miss M struggled out of the chair and hobbled over to the desk, pushed up the roll-top and rummaged about in the compartments at the back. Eventually, she produced a card, now yellowed with age, which she handed to Anna. 'This is their number.'

'How long will all this take?'

'Usually a few months to get a counselling appointment, then you have to wait a couple more for the certificate to arrive. By the way, when is your birthday?'

Anna watched as Miss M wrote down the date then said, 'But even if I get the certificate I still won't know where she's living now.'

'No, but there are ways of finding out. The adoption agency can tell you more about that. But if you do find her, will you promise me something?'

'What?'

'You won't try to contact her. You'll get someone else to

do it for you. Just in case things don't work out as you hope.'

'Would you do that for me?'

'Of course, dear.'

***

Anna hit the end of the rush hour and had to stand until Warren Street. Hardly worth sitting down for the remaining two stops. But her luck was in at St Pancras. The board announced a train for Nottingham in fifteen minutes. She just had time to go to the kiosk, ask for a coffee and pick up the first sandwich she saw. She didn't care what was in it.

In a seat next to the window, she removed the lid from the cardboard cup. The flaps, folded flat round the sides, were useless when bent back to form a handle, so she cradled the cup in her hands, drawing a little comfort from its warmth. The sandwich was tuna. She hated tuna. The slimy filling stuck on her tongue, but she persevered. She'd only had a pear drop and a chocolate biscuit since breakfast.

She stared out of the window at the reflection of the passenger sitting opposite superimposed on the flashing images of gardens and houses backing onto the track. She guessed the woman was in her late thirties, the age her mother would be now. Oh, this was ridiculous: She couldn't spend the rest of her life imagining every middle-aged woman she came across might be her mother.

CHAPTER 13

"Always on my mind"
Pet Shop Boys 1987

Valerie stared across the pea-green ripples of Long Water and hunched her neck further down into her woollen scarf. Seagulls and cormorants perched on the posts that formed the chain-linked barrier across this stretch of the Serpentine. In the summer, when the children were younger, she'd bring them here to Kensington Gardens: she could picture them now standing at the railings breaking the stale crusts into bits and throwing them to the Canada geese, the mallard ducks and the little black coots. Alison, her eldest, had known the names of all the water fowl and had recorded her sightings in an *I Spy* book. When all the bread was gone the two younger children would run back across the path to the famous statue. Lucy would attempt to climb up, the leather soles of her buckled shoes slipping on the bronze worn smooth by generations of tiny feet. She never made it up to where a miniature Wendy hung on gazing adoringly at Peter Pan, who stood at the top playing a tune on a magical pipe that curved upwards to the sky. Katy, the youngest of Valerie's children, would be at the bottom of the statue pointing to the verdigris-encrusted creatures saying 'fawies, squiwel, mouses, wabbit, dickey bird.'

But that had been years ago: now Alison was eighteen, in her first year at university, Lucy would leave next year to train as a nurse. Only Katy would be left at home and in a couple of years she too would be gone. Then it would be just her and Brian with no one to fill the widening gap that was developing between them. And there'd be more time to think.

She stared again at the statue, the bronze memorial to Never Never Land. On this cold December day, no children had been brought to see it, to be told the story of the boy who never grew up. But all children did grow up. Almost three weeks ago on 22 November it had been her son, Brian's, twenty-first birthday. Had there been a party: champagne and cake? Did his other mother organise it or perhaps his wife? For all she knew he could be married now, she could even be a grandmother.

Valerie rummaged in her handbag for the photo taken in Susan's small attic room at *The House*: the four of them arms round each other, faces with false smiles leaning forward into the lens of the camera. If you looked closely you could see the red rims round Susan's eyes, because it was taken the day she left, the day she gave little Chloe away. On the back of the photo in Susan's handwriting was today's date. Would the other three come? Would they remember about this reunion? Would the photograph have been lost, discarded with other baggage of their past life? After all it was way back in 1966 that the letter from Susan with the four Christmas cards and four photographs inside had arrived at *The House*.

And if they did come, what would she say to them? They would all have changed, become different people. The ties of shame and sorrow that had once bound them together would long ago have unravelled. Maybe Brian was right. This was a bad idea. She shouldn't have come.

'Hiya, Valerie.'

She stared at the woman who was waving and running towards her. The face was familiar, but somehow different.

Then she realized what was missing. There were no false eyelashes, not a trace of backcombing. 'Paula.'

'Thought I was gonna be late.' Paula sat down on the bench to catch her breath. 'Didn't recognise me, did you? I'd have known you anywhere. You look just the same.'

Surely not: she wasn't a size 18 back then. Valerie put her hand to her newly-permed hair. When she'd asked Brian if it was an improvement, he'd just said, 'Uh Uh' and carried on putting the finishing touches to his matchstick model of Blackpool tower.

'It's great to see you.' Paula looked at her watch. 'Five past eleven. D'you think the others are coming?'

'Susan should. After all she arranged this get-together.'

'Well I've gorra say it's a stupid place to choose. A park in the middle of winter.'

'At least she could be sure it would still be here, unless someone chose to dig it up to build more skyscraper flats.' Valerie gazed around: just trees, not a building in sight. 'It's amazing don't you think. You'd never know you were in the centre of London. It's so peaceful.'

'And bloody cold.'

Stilettos clicked on the path; a woman was heading towards them. She wore knee-high boots and a red coat with a fur collar.

As she drew closer Paula stood up and muttered. 'Ger a load o' that.'

Susan threw her arms round Paula. 'You made it. That's wonderful. How are you? And Valerie. You look just the same.'

Valerie inhaled a hint of Christian Dior as Susan leaned forward, pursed her lips and placed her cheek next to hers. Surprised by this sudden display of affection, Valerie stepped back and said, 'We're only waiting for Gwyneth now. Do you think she'll come?'

'Didn't seem too keen.' Paula shrugged. 'When we got the letter.'

'But then neither did you,' Valerie reminded her.

'Well you never forget somethin' like that do you … giving your baby away.' Paula took a packet of Superkings from her bag and flipped open the top. 'Here let's have a ciggie and if she's not here by the time we've finished it, we'll go.'

Susan took one.

Valerie hesitated then did the same. 'I don't often smoke, but today's different isn't it?'

'So, where have you two come from?' asked Susan.

'Oh, I'm still in South London,' said Valerie.

'I went back to Liverpool.' Paula smiled. 'Once a scouser, always a scouser.'

'Last time I heard …' Valerie coughed as the smoke hit the back of her throat. '… you were working in Harrods.'

'Was there about six months. Then one day I told me best friend about Gina. Some friend! Thought I could trust her. Next day it was all round the store that I'd had a baby and from then on everyone kinda looked at me different, like, specially the fellas. So, I told them what they could do with their job. What about Gwyneth. Did she go back to Wales?'

Valerie looked away to where a flight of geese skimmed across the water. 'I don't know. After I left *The House,* I never heard from any of you again.'

Paula dropped her cigarette stub on the path and flattened it under the sole of her shoe. 'Well, I reckon she's not coming.'

'If we make our way up to Lancaster Gate Tube station, there's a café not too far away,' said Susan.

The three of them walked back along the path towards the park entrance. Gusts of wind caught the fountains in the Italian gardens bending the jets of water and showering them with a spray of icy droplets. Valerie tried to cover her hair with her hands.

'That's nor 'er is it?' Paula pointed to a figure in a tweed coat, hurrying in through the gates.

'Must be.' Susan rushed forward to hug their old friend.

'There is good to see you, it is,' said Gwyneth.

Paula and Susan ordered coffee, Valerie and Gwyneth asked for tea. Valerie chose a meringue, Paula a chocolate éclair and Gwyneth a custard tart. Susan resisted temptation, saying she was watching her weight, although Valerie was sure she couldn't be more than a size 10.

At first no one spoke of their time at *The House*. Instead Paula and Gwyneth exchanged complaints about their long train journeys and compared notes about where they'd stayed the night before: Gwyneth in a B&B in South Kensington, Paula in a hotel near Sloane Square.

Then Valerie could stand the small talk no longer. 'They took him away you know … little Brian.'

The other three girls exchanged glances.

Gwyneth was the first to speak. 'We didn't know, see. Didn't know why we never saw you again. We did ask Miss M for your address, mind, but she wouldn't give it to us, said it would be best for the new girls if we didn't talk about what had happened.'

'I went back to see Miss M, you know, when they let me out.' Valerie avoided eye-contact. 'Out of the hospital, but it was too late. My mother had already signed the adoption papers. The doctors had said I wasn't in a fit state of mind.'

'There is terrible. What about your boyfriend, Brian? What did he do?'

'What could he do? They wouldn't even tell him where little Brian was fostered. The court said a seventeen-year old lad couldn't look after a baby and his mam had too many children already.'

'But you're married now.' Paula nodded towards the ring on the third finger of Valerie's left hand.

'Brian and I went to the registry office the day I was eighteen, three months before our second baby was born. We've got three children now. All girls. Brian has a good job and we almost own a three-bedroom semi in Tooting.'

Susan looked round the table. 'So, all our babies were adopted?'

'I was gonna keep Gina.' Paula looked down at her coffee, parting the surface froth with her teaspoon. 'Always thought I shoulda tried harder, put up with a grotty flat until I'd saved up, like.'

'But it wouldn't have been easy for any of us,' said Susan.

'And I wouldn't have been able to go back to Liverpool, 'cos I've never told anyone back home about the baby. If I had then Dave would never have married me and I wouldn't have had our Michelle and our Richard.'

Gwyneth looked at Susan and asked, 'You married too?' When Susan nodded, she added, 'So it's only me not married, then.'

'You went back to Wales?' asked Susan.

'Yes, trained as a teacher, then went home to Anglesey to work in the infants' school.'

'Must be hard teaching other people's children, when you gave your own baby away.'

'Sad it is, sad indeed how some parents bring up their children: let them play in the street while they're drinking in the pub. The poor little ones come to school in unwashed clothes and fall asleep on their desks. These people don't deserve them, they don't. I pray to God that Eirlys went to a family who care for her properly.'

'Miss M told me that little Brian would be all right. The agencies always inspect the families to make sure they're suitable,' said Valerie. 'They have rules like they must go to church regularly.'

'These religious biddies are the worst,' said Paula.

Valerie cringed and looked across at Gwyneth but she didn't appear to have heard.

'I try not to think about Eirlys. Keep busy. There's Band of Hope on Tuesday night, choir practice on Thursday. Only every year on her birthday I buy a card. For the last few years, I've bought a half bottle of gin to drink while I write it. There is nonsense for you, buying a card I'll never be able to post.'

'But you might be able to one day,' said Valerie. 'Adopted children can now find out who their real mothers are, come and find us.'

'Doesn't work the other way round, though. We can't search for our children.' Susan sighed. 'But I have written a letter and sent it to the adoption agency in case Chloe comes looking for me.'

'But didn't you know *Families Forever* has closed down?'

'Oh no! 'When? Why?'

'A few years ago. Not as many babies go for adoption these days,' said Valerie. 'I've sent my letter to Social Services instead.'

'But I don't want Eirlys to find me.'

'Really?' Susan and Valerie stared at Gwyneth in disbelief.

'A new family she has now but I'll never forget her.'

Susan nodded. 'No, you never forget. You may put it to the back of your mind for a short while, but then something quite trivial will come back to remind you. The other day on the Tube a woman was knitting: something small in pink wool. I had to get off one stop early so the other passengers wouldn't see me crying.'

'But you got married.'

'Yes, in 1969. Pictures were in *The Tatler.*'

'That's class. You must have been made up? How did you meet him?' asked Paula. 'Rich, is he?'

Susan told them how after she left *The House,* she stayed at home for a few months but got very bored and kept falling out with her parents, so she came back to London and got a job in an art gallery on the Kings Road. Two years later she married the owner, a widower in his thirties with two children at boarding school.

'Did you tell him about your baby?'

'Geoffrey said it didn't matter. We could still have a white wedding.'

'Did you have any more children?'

Susan rolled her earring between her thumb and forefinger. 'No. Being stepmother to two boys, seven and eight was enough.'

'Are they still at home?' asked Valerie.

'Good gracious me, no. The eldest is a solicitor. The other one is off "finding himself" in India. Rings home when he needs money.'

Conversation drifted back to *The House.* Everyone had fond memories of Miss M.

'I don't know how she put up with us,' said Valerie.

Paula smiled. 'D'you remember how Nina carried her baby around everywhere and in the end Miss M said she could bring him with her to the table at meal times.'

'Really,' said Susan. 'I never saw her baby. She was still down at Florrie's when I left the house. Did anyone keep in touch with her?'

'I did,' said Paula. 'Went to see her when I was still working at Harrods. She was living in this bed-sit. The house was a dump, smelled of dirty nappies. The landlady looked after the babies while the mums went to work, but when Nina heard how they cried all day she wouldn't leave her little boy so she didn't have a job, was still living on the social.'

'So, what happened to her?'

Paula shrugged. 'Never saw her again. Meant to. But then I packed in my job and went back to Liverpool. Yer know how it is?'

'Well I suppose we've all moved on. Left that part of our life behind. But it wasn't fair was it? What they did to us. It would never happen today.' Susan sighed. 'Anyway, I must be going.' She pushed back her chair and got up. 'I'm meeting Geoffrey and we're going for dinner then on to the theatre.'

They said goodbye to Susan outside the café as the black cab she'd hailed drew up at the curb. She got into the back and blew kisses through the window as it pulled out into the rush-hour traffic.

'Well it's the Tube for the likes of us,' said Paula. "Are you going to Euston too, Gwyneth?'

'Yes, there is a train just after six.'

'I was thinking of getting that one,' said Paula. 'We could

travel together as far as Crewe if you like.'

They took the Central line and changed at Tottenham Court Road where Valerie led the way through the maze of tunnels to the Northern line.

As the train drew into the northbound platform she said, 'I'll come up to Euston with you.'

Paula frowned. 'But you're going south.'

'I know, but I'm in no hurry,' said Valerie. There's nothing I need to get home for.'

The three of them sat side by side on the Tube, Gwyneth in the middle.

'Well Susan's done alright for herself. Did yer see those rings? And those earrings. D'yer reckon those diamonds were real?'

'Of course.' said Gwyneth. 'But did you see her face, Valerie, when you were talking about your children?'

'Yea.' Paula nodded. 'She did look kinda sad. But she said she didn't want no more children. Two stepsons were quite enough.'

'But it's not the same,' Gwyneth said. 'They're not her children.'

Valerie had hoped there'd be time for a cup of tea in the station buffet. She still hadn't shown the others the photos of her three daughters. When they arrived at Euston, however, the train for Crewe was already in and due to leave in ten minutes.

Paula hugged her. 'Great to see yer again, Valerie.'

Gwyneth smiled and squeezed her hand. 'I'm glad to know you and Brian are married and have more children.'

***

There was plenty of time to think on the Tube down to Tooting Bec. The meeting Valerie had looked forward to for months was over. In the weeks leading up to it, she'd tried to imagine what the others would be like now, but twenty-one years had cast a shadow over what they'd all once been. Each girl had trodden their own path: Gwyneth, still on her own, had filled the emptiness with a career, devoting her life to thirty different five-year-olds every year. Paula hosted Tupperware parties in her detached house and took holidays on the Costa del Sol, Susan organised art exhibitions and struggled to come to terms with the fact that she was now a step-grandmother.

What had they all thought of her? Right now, on the train, her old friends were probably saying that, apart from not having little Brian, Valerie had everything she wanted. Until a few years ago she would probably have agreed. That was when she started looking at other men. At first, she just considered eligible males on the telly: what would they be like to go out with, to live with, as lovers? When Brian made love to her – not very often now – she imagined he was someone else. She told herself this was just because there'd never been anyone else. How could she not be curious?

She still loved him and she was sure that he still loved her, but as life had become less of a struggle, for her anyway, it had become boring. What was there to look forward to? Becoming old? She was only thirty-seven, but life was passing her by.

Would she spend her life waiting, waiting for the day little Brian came to look for her, thinking it might be him each time that the phone rang or a letter dropped on the doormat? Her husband knew how she hoped, how she waited, but didn't say anything, except about the reunion. He'd tried to persuade her not to go, said it would just open old wounds, send her back into the place where he couldn't reach her. But no, she wasn't going back there to that black hole, that vicious circle of happy pills and sleeping tablets. It was more than twenty years now since she'd climbed out and kept busy, first with school work then after her marriage cooking and cleaning, making packed lunches and driving back and forth to Brownies and ballet.

Sometimes Valerie wondered what she would have done if she hadn't become pregnant at fifteen. Would she have stayed with Brian or would some more interesting lad have come along? Would she have gone on to university? She was clever enough, she knew that. After the "unfortunate incident", as her mother had insisted on calling it, was over, she'd gone back to school and got eight GCEs, enough to go on and do "A" levels. But what her mother didn't know was that by taking one baby away all her daughter could think about was having another. She never intended to stay on in the sixth form, because on her first day she already knew she was pregnant again and on her eighteenth birthday she and Brian would get married.

The wedding was a quiet affair. Valerie's parents wouldn't have come even if they had been invited. When her legitimate grandchild was born, Mrs Johnson came around with presents, but the tiny dresses she bought were never worn, still had the price tags on when Valerie donated them to the charity shop years later. It was Brian's mum and dad that the girls called Nan and Grandad.

It was last September that she started to wonder what she would do with the rest of her life. When they'd left Alison, their eldest, at the halls of residence Valerie couldn't help thinking "this could have been me". Social work, that's what she'd wanted to do. What a laugh, after what social workers had done to her. No, they didn't call them social workers then; it was moral welfare workers. But things were different now: the policy was not to condemn and wrench mothers and babies apart but to help keep them together.

But she couldn't, could she? She couldn't start a career at her age. But then why not? There was another twenty-three years before she reached retirement age. The thought of filling more than two decades with WI meetings and cleaning a house that was already clean didn't bear thinking about.

When she got home, Brian was waiting, a look of concern on his face. 'How did it go?'

'Everyone came.' Valerie went through to the kitchen calling over her shoulder, 'The others, they've never seen their babies again either.'

'You didn't get too upset, then?'

She came back into the living room with two mugs of tea. 'No, it's sad though hearing how they miss their babies too.'

'So, have they all got married, had other children?

'Paula has. Susan has step-children. That must be hard when you know you've given your own child away.'

'And Gwyneth?'

'No, Gwyneth never got married. She has her career. You know I've been thinking about what would have happened if I'd never got pregnant with little Brian. Would I have gone to college, university even? Would I have a career?'

'But you always said you enjoyed looking after the children.'

'Yes, but Katy's getting older, doesn't really need me much now. Perhaps I should think of getting a job, going to college even.'

CHAPTER 14

"Sweet Child o' Mine"
Guns N' Roses 1988

'Samaritans. How may I help you?'

No reply.

'You're through to the Samaritans.'

A faint sound of sobbing.

'Perhaps you're finding it difficult to talk?'

'Yes.'

'Take your time.'

More sobs.

'I'm still here for you.'

'It's over twenty years now, since … I gave my baby away.'

Susan closed her eyes, breathed in, swallowed hard and willed herself not to cry. Mothering Sunday. She knew she shouldn't have come in. But the rota organiser said that none of the other volunteers could make it and, in the end, she'd agreed. It had been just as she'd feared: several of the calls were from mothers: mothers whose children had died, mothers whose children were missing, mothers whose children had forgotten what day it was. Then came the call she'd most dreaded: a woman who, like herself, had given her baby away.

The feelings this caller expressed were so similar to those Susan had endured for more than twenty-one years, but the Samaritans' policy forbidding self-disclosure meant that she couldn't admit to suffering the same guilt and regret. Her only outlet was silent tears which she kept in check and wiped away with a finger as she listened to this all-too-familiar story. After three quarters of an hour the caller hung up. Susan replaced the receiver, lay back in her chair and exhaled.

The leader-on-duty came over and put his hand on Susan's shoulder. 'You OK?'

'Too close to home?'

'Do you want to talk?'

'Not now.'

'After we've finished the shift?'

Susan nodded.

They made coffee in the cramped kitchen and took it through to the de-briefing room, where they settled themselves in easy chairs, new cushions covering the threadbare upholstery.

Susan gave a resumé of the four calls she had taken, leaving the most difficult till last.

'She said she wasn't suicidal, just wanted to tell someone about it. Kept saying, "You wouldn't understand", but I did.'

'So, what did you say?'

'Didn't have to say much, just listened while she poured it all out. At the end she thanked me and said she felt better.'

'That's good, but how about you, how do you feel? You said it was too close to home.'

'I once rang the Samaritans with a very similar story.

The leader nodded as he replaced his coffee mug on the low table and leant forward. 'Is that why you decided to become a volunteer?'

Susan nodded. 'I thought maybe I could help someone else, like the lady I spoke to years ago helped me.'

'So, you felt she helped you back then?'

'Well, it didn't change anything, but she was there for me when I needed someone.' Susan took a sip of black coffee. 'I was seventeen when I gave my daughter up for adoption. I thought if I kept her no other man would ever want me; I'd never get married. And anyway, I couldn't possibly look after a baby on my own. But giving her away was much harder than I thought it would be.'

'Like the caller you've just spoken to?'

'You think you've got over it but you haven't. It's always there at the back of your mind. When she was little, I'd be in town and I'd see old ladies cooing over prams, babies grinning back and wonder: did my baby have her first tooth? In the park I'd see tiny tots, their hands reaching up, clinging on, as they staggered in front of their mothers across the grass, and wonder if my daughter had taken her first steps.'

'I can't begin to imagine how hard that must be.'

'As she grew up, I'd look at children in supermarket trolleys or coming out of school gates and pick out the ones with fair hair and blue eyes. Was she mine? Then I'd remember that when I last saw Chloe, her hair was more mousey than fair, and all babies have blue eyes when they're born. I'd remind myself that if ever I did come across my little girl, I'd not recognise her.'

Susan hesitated. Why was she telling all this to a man she hardly knew? But it was OK, being a Samaritan, she knew none of this would go any further.

'Birthdays are the worst. Last year when she was twenty-one, I met up with some of the other girls from the home where our babies were born. They all feel the same. One of them is trying to find her baby.'

'And you?'

***

'What number?' asked the taxi driver.

Susan took a tissue from her handbag, to wipe away the mist coating the inside of the window. She peered through the mist-free circle at the dull April afternoon, not so much different from that bleak November day she could never forget: the same drab houses, pavements with empty cigarette packets and crisp bags scurrying along in the wind. Then she was in her father's car, a pale-faced, mini-skirted teenager with hair hanging loose down her back, putting on a brave face as she headed home to piece together the remnants of her pre-pregnancy life. Now she was coming back, a woman in her early forties, her skin tanned in the Caribbean, her hair still long but now swept up and pinned into a French pleat, diamonds and sapphires sparkling on the third and fourth fingers of both hands. And once again she was putting on a brave face.

'It's alright, just drop me here at the bottom of Granby Hill.' Even after all these years Susan didn't want anyone to know of her connection with number 13, *The House*.

'That'll be three-pound twenty.'

Susan handed the driver a five-pound note. 'Keep the change.'

She couldn't believe it. Numbers 1, 3, 5 and 7 were just rubble. Where 9 and 11 had once been, floral wallpaper was exposed to the elements, staircases rose up into nothing. Only two houses remained intact: 13 and 15.

Men in hard hats whistled as she walked up the hill.

'You all right, luv?'

She hadn't seen him approach: the man in the torn and dusty overalls.

'Yes. Yes, thank you.'

He started to move away.

'Do you know?' she called after him. 'Does anyone still live at number 13?'

He smiled. 'You mean the old dear. She keeps bringing us cups of tea and asking if we can make a little less noise.' He snorted. 'I don't know how we're supposed to demolish houses quietly.'

As if to emphasise his point, there was a crack and a rumble, as the heavy metal ball swung in an arc and hit yet another wall, and bricks cascaded to the ground.

'She's only there till the end of the month. We start on these last two, first week in May.'

More than twenty years had taken its toll. Even back then, in 1966, *The House of Help* had begun its slow decline, but now it had given up any pretence of its former Victorian grandeur. The brickwork was crumbling, weeds thrived in the blocked guttering. The stained-glass windows were cracked, the holes blocked up with cardboard.

Susan walked past the stone gate-posts, with only rusty hinges to indicate where gates had once been, up the drive where gravel had given way to bare earth and potholes, around Miss M's rose bed, now just a tangle of briars and ground elder. Half-hidden in the undergrowth was a sign: the words *FOR SALE* only just visible.

A buddleia had taken root in a crack in the steps, and drooped over the stone balustrade. At the top Susan hesitated. Flaking paintwork revealed the rotten wood of the double front door. This was the house that had once sucked her in then, three months later, spewed her out, changed forever. She pulled the long wrought-iron handle and from inside came the sound that she hadn't heard for more than twenty-one years; but even now the jangle of that ancient bell could still make her cry.

'Just a minute,' said a voice from inside.

The old dear the workman had mentioned couldn't be Miss M, could it?

When the door opened, there she was, still wearing Crimplene and cardigans, but stooped, now supporting herself with one hand pressing down on an aluminium walking stick with three legs.

'Miss M, I didn't think you'd still be here, not after all this time.'

'So, you must be …' Miss M peered through lenses, much thicker than the ones she used to wear. 'Now let me think …'

'It's Susan.'

'Well I never, Susan. What a surprise. Your young man, he was a GI, wasn't he?'

How amazing the old lady should remember that.

'Come on in.' Miss M turned and led the way into the office.

The oak panelling in the hall was now shrouded in dust, the stair-rods tarnished: no army of girls to do the dusting and polishing any more.

The office still smelled of ashes-of-violets cologne and pear drops. Nothing had changed: the roll-top desk was still piled high with papers, a bottle of vodka waited on the window sill, now no attempt to hide it behind the curtain. The only new addition was a birdcage with a blue and grey budgerigar asleep on its perch.

'Sit yourself down.' Miss M pointed to the armchair that every girl who had ever lived at *The House* had sat in, most of them pouring out their heart to this lady who listened and said very little and never, never passed judgement.

'How did you know who I was?'

'I can't remember all my girls, of course. There were so many, but you I remember because you always said you wanted a white wedding. Did you have one?'

'Yes.'

'And children?'

'No.'

Miss M reached over and put her hand over Susan's.

'No, I never had another baby of my own.' Susan looked away and stared at the gas fire as it flickered from blue to orange. 'We tried. Even the best gynaecologist that money could buy couldn't help. We knew it wasn't my husband, because he already had two children, was a widower, you see, when I met him.'

'But you. You'd had a child too.'

'I know. The doctor said that maybe when my baby was born something happened to make me infertile. What do you think?'

'I don't know, dear. I was never told about anything that went on down at Florrie's. But you say you have step-children.'

'It's not the same. They remember their real mother, not me, on Mother's Day. And anyway, they were both away at boarding school when we got married. I so wanted a baby, a baby of my own, because I could never forget the baby I gave away.'

'I know, dear.'

'You've got a photo of Chloe up there.' Susan got up and went over to the notice-board. 'And there's Valerie holding her baby and Paula with Gina, not one of Gwyneth though.'

'No, she asked me not to take one.'

'She was odd was Gwyneth. Never talked about her baby's father, her family or anything. When we all met up earlier this year, around the time of our baby's twenty-first birthdays, she hadn't married and said how she still thought of her daughter.'

'I remember she called her Eirlys, such a pretty name.'

'But she said if ever her daughter came looking for her, she'd refuse to see her. I couldn't understand that.'

'Gwyneth has her reasons and, believe me, she cares a great deal about Eirlys. Anyway, I'm so pleased to hear you met up. Never thought you would. You'd all have new lives. You wouldn't forget, you just wouldn't have time.'

'Valerie told us what happened to her. It was awful, wasn't it?'

'Unforgivable.'

'She married Brian though.'

'I know. She used to come and see me. Wanted to find little Brian so he could come back to live with his real mum and dad, his new sisters, but of course that was impossible.'

'Do you think you'd be able to help me find Chloe?'

'I thought that's why you'd come.' Miss M reached for her stick and pushed herself to her feet. 'Now let's make a nice cup of tea and then we'll talk about it.'

In the kitchen the only concession that Miss M had made to the passage of time was a microwave, which stood in pristine newness between the fifties-style fridge and the cast-iron cooker.

As they waited for the extra-large kettle to boil, Susan thought perhaps she should leave pursuing the topic of tracing her daughter until they were back in the office, so she said, 'One of the workmen told me you were moving out soon.'

'Yes, I would probably have done so before this, if it hadn't been for Le-Roy.'

'Who is Le-Roy?'

'You remember Christine?'

'I don't think so.'

'She cooked Christmas dinner.'

'I left the second week in November.'

'Ah, she wouldn't have been here then, because she had her baby on Christmas Day, and it was early. She called him Le-Roy after his father. He was from Jamaica.'

'So, you said you couldn't leave.' Susan looked puzzled. 'Because of Le-Roy.'

'He lives here, you see.'

'But he must be in his twenties by now?'

'Yes. You see, when he was a baby he stayed here while the agency tried to find a family to adopt him. He could have been fostered, of course, but Christine wouldn't hear of it. Then cook retired and so Christine took over in the kitchen till we found a replacement. It was amazing: that girl could hardly read a word, but she could cook. When no-one applied for the job I persuaded the Ladies on the Committee to give it to Christine.'

'And Le-Roy stayed too?'

'He was what they called a "hard to place" baby, but such a lovely little chap, he's grown up into a fine young man.'

'But didn't they have to leave when this place stopped being a mother and baby home?'

'Where could they go? I just didn't mention to anyone that they were still here. When the Ladies on the Committee tried to sell the house, there was some problem with a clause in Mr Arlington-Smythe's Will, which held up the sale. And while the lawyers argued they forgot all about us.'

'But it's been sold now?'

'Yes, and they're knocking it down. Good job too. Too

many tears have been shed in this house.'

'Where will you go?'

'I've a nice little flat lined up.'

'And Christine?'

'Christine died. She was ill for a long time. Heart trouble, you know. We looked after her best we could. At the end Le-Roy gave up his job to be with her. But London Transport has taken him back now. He's got a girlfriend and they've found a flat. They say they'll live together for a while then, maybe, get married.'

As they walked back up the hall, Susan carrying the tea tray, a voice inside the office screeched, 'Stop banging. Stop banging.'

She looked at Miss M.

The old lady smiled and pushed open the door. 'You don't want to mind Percy. He just gets very upset with all the noise the demolition men are making.'

'Oh, I see, the budgie.' Susan saw that the bird in the cage was now wide awake and sharpening his beak on a cuttlefish bone.

'Be quiet now, Percy, I need to talk to this lady about her baby.'

***

Susan picked her way carefully down the drive, her emotions in turmoil, but still taking care not to splash mud from the potholes onto her suede court shoes. As she turned onto the road, she waved to Miss M who was still watching from the doorway. Once out of sight she slowed down, reluctant to go home, back to the silent house she'd left with such high hopes only that morning.

At the bottom of the hill she hailed a taxi. It was now after five. As they crawled a few yards, then stopped again, hemmed in by the rush-hour traffic she looked out of the window, as usual searching for fair-haired, blue-eyed young women among passengers in hooting cars and pedestrians pushing their way through the crowds on the pavement. It seemed now that the chances of ever finding her daughter were very slim.

Back in the mid-seventies there'd been the heated debate about whether adopted children had the right to know who their birth parents were. When the act was passed allowing them access to their original birth certificates, her daughter had been ten years old. Then it was another seven long years before Chloe would be able to come looking for her birth mother. However, a few months before her daughter was eighteen Susan had written to the *Families Forever* adoption agency with her contact details. October 3rd 1984 came and went and there was no letter, no phone call. That was the day Susan had first phoned the Samaritans.

On the outside, it appeared that Susan had everything: a five-bedroom house in four acres of ground, a husband who obviously adored her, but something was missing. All the things money could buy she could have, so, if she was never going to find her daughter, what was there to aim for? Where did she go from here? What was the point of going on?

Then at the reunion Valerie had told her that *Families Forever* had closed down and Susan's hopes soared. The reason her daughter hadn't found her was because there was no one to pass on her letter. She had written again, this time to Social Services. Then she had waited.

That afternoon Susan had cried there at *The House*, just as she had more than twenty-one years earlier, 'If only, if only I'd never given Chloe away.'

'Don't blame yourself,' Miss M had said. 'Back then it was hard for single mothers. You did what you had to for the sake of your baby, to give her two parents, a comfortable life.'

But this hadn't made Susan feel any better. She hadn't been there to cuddle her little girl when she scraped her knees, to guide her teenage daughter though the hormone-fuelled roller-coaster of adolescence, for that woman to woman chat when she had her first period...

... to warn her that the first stirrings of passion aren't always love.

CHAPTER 15

"Wish me luck as you wave me goodbye"
Gracie Fields 1940

Miss M stood in the doorway until Susan was out of sight. Should she have told her that it was possible that her grown-up daughter had visited *The House* a few years ago? No, best not to say anything, not to get Susan's hopes up until she was sure and had checked with Chloe. No, that wasn't her name now. What was it her adoptive parents had christened her?

Back in the office, Miss M pushed up the top of the roll-top desk and sighed at the untidy pile of paperwork. The address and telephone number the girl had left, just in case Miss M heard from her mother, must be here somewhere amidst the clutter. Exhausted by the day's excitement and finding it harder to focus in the fading light, Miss M decided that it would be much easier to find the scrap of paper in the morning.

It wasn't often she drank these days; the doctor had said she should cut down. But then it wasn't every day that there was a chance that she might be able to reunite one of her girls with their baby. So, she poured herself a small tot from the vodka bottle, replaced it on the windowsill before lowering herself into the armchair next to the fire and leaning forward to turn the gas down to miser rate.

Susan had come just in time. In three weeks, *The House of Help* would be reduced to rubble: all traces of the institution, created to scoop up the flotsam washed up by past tides of intolerance, would be gone. For almost thirty

167

years she had lived here with girls who had nowhere to go, or needed to conceal their condition from those only too willing to condemn.

It wasn't only the girls that had a secret: Miss M, herself, had a secret, a secret she only ever shared with mothers who decided to keep their babies, and then only in a few moments alone with them in her office before they left. She hoped by knowing that back in 1940 she too had given birth to a child out of wedlock and brought him up on her own might in some way sustain them as unmarried mothers in an unsympathetic world.

***

It was the war: how could she let the man she loved go back to the front, without giving him the comfort and the memories he needed? If she hadn't, he would have died never knowing real love and passion. James had been stationed at army barracks not far from where she lived. They'd met at the church where her father had been vicar, before he became ill. A spinster at thirty, she'd given up hope of finding a suitor, but there they were walking out together. People they passed would turn around for a second look. Perhaps they realised he was five years younger than she was, but what did it matter? She loved him: his curly, fair hair tamed by a short back and sides, his brown eyes sometimes distant when he recalled the horrors of war, the fleeting smile that crossed his lips when, for a moment, he forgot what he was going back to.

He had wanted to marry her, but she said no, not now, with her father's health failing. They'd postpone the wedding till later when she had no responsibilities and the war was over. How she was to regret that decision. Marriage would have meant she was a war widow struggling to bring up a child on a war pension. As it was, she became a single woman who, after an irresponsible wartime affair, was expecting a child with no means of supporting it. Fortunately, her father had been spared the knowledge that his unmarried daughter was with child: he passed away before her condition became obvious.

***

Miss M raised her eyes to the photograph on the mantelpiece: herself in her best costume and a matching hat with a feather, James in his khaki uniform above polished boots, standing to attention. She'd written to tell him that she was carrying his child, but she'd never know if he received the letter before he perished on the beach at Dunkirk.

The roar of the bulldozers and crash of falling masonry had stopped: the demolition workers must have gone home. Now there was silence. Even Percy was asleep, balanced on his perch, his head tucked beneath his wing. Miss M closed her eyes and replayed in her head the past sounds of *The House*: the tiny whimpering cries of the new-borns, the demanding screams of the bonny six-weekers; she inhaled past aromas of National Dried Milk and Johnson's baby powder.

***

There had been no *House of Help* when her baby son, James, was born. At her father's funeral she'd confided in an aunt who offered to take her in for her confinement. The arrangement cost a generous amount out of her meagre inheritance but where else was there for her to go?

As the grey winter landscape gave way to lush green, she watched her baby's limbs plump out, his eyes change from blue to brown like his father's. He would turn his head at

169

her voice and give her a big toothless smile. As she pushed a borrowed pram through the village, passers-by would stop to admire such a pretty baby. In the morning while he slept, she didn't mind pounding away with the posser, trying to get the shirts and sheets in the peggy-tub whiter than white, getting down on her knees to scour the kitchen floor.

But she knew then it couldn't last. James's cries in the night were disturbing her uncle, and the neighbours were asking why her husband didn't come home on leave: had they noticed she wasn't wearing a wedding ring?

'There's a couple in the village can't have children,' her aunt had said.

She spent many sleepless nights trying to decide what to do. She'd get up in the morning thinking he'd be better off with two parents, but by evening she knew there was no way she could be parted from her son. A week later she'd bought a brass wedding ring from Woolworths and started looking for somewhere more permanent to live.

***

'Chin up. Chin up.'

Miss M woke with a start and looked over to where the budgie was squawking at her from behind the bars of his cage.

'Hush now, Percy.'

She bent down to rub her knee, before getting up to switch on the light and draw the curtains. Then she returned to her chair: she'd sit a while before making the tea.

***

Those years at the beginning of the war were hard for everyone, but especially for women on their own with children. A bedsit at the top of three flights of stairs was all she could afford and the small amount of money she had left wouldn't pay even the seven shillings and sixpence rent for very long. Porridge, bread and potatoes was what she survived on; there was no need to buy food for her baby who was still suckling. Then the newspaper placards said women were needed to help the war effort, even those with children, as the new day and night nurseries would provide childcare while mothers went out to work.

The munitions factory paid one pound eighteen shillings a week. At first James cried when she left him, all day he refused milk from a teat or food from a spoon and latched on to her breast as soon as they got home. She began to wonder if she had made the right choice: would her son be better off back there in the village with the couple who couldn't have children? Then she'd see a faint hint of his father flit across baby James's face and she would know that, however much harder things became, she would never give him up.

For four years she filled shell cases at the munitions factory. Then the war was over. A week after VE Day, the nursery closed down: there was no need for factories making weapons any more. The servicemen came home to their wives and their jobs: there was little work for women, especially single women with children.

***

Time was getting on: she couldn't just sit here reminiscing, but it seemed such an effort to make tea just for herself; tonight, Le-Roy would have something to eat at his girlfriend's. In the kitchen she opened the fridge and looked under the upturned soup bowl: 'Good lad.' He'd opened the can of corned beef just as she'd asked him. It was there neatly sliced on the plate. She carried it across to the kitchen table, then went back for a tomato and the margarine. When it was all laid out before her, together with a slice from the ready-cut loaf and a piece of Battenberg cake, she sat down. How she hated eating alone.

***

Even during those war years in that tiny bedsitter there had been James to share her meals with, however limited their conversations had been at first. By the time he was three he could tell her halting tales of his day at nursery.

In the summer of 1945, their life had changed and, from then on, she'd never eaten alone … not until now. Her salvation had been *The Lady*: she'd scour the situations vacant columns, looking for people who wanted housekeepers or live-in maids or companions. Most of the letters of application she wrote didn't even get a reply. Then when the money in the Post Office savings book was down to five pounds there was a family looking for a housekeeper and it actually said child welcome.

She wrote the letter, re-read it then screwed it up and started again and so it went on, through several drafts. How could she waste the Basildon Bond that had made such a hole in her savings? But somehow, somehow, she had to make them offer her this position, so, for the first and last time in her life, she lied. She was the daughter of a vicar, had looked after a six-bedroom vicarage since her mother died when she was fourteen, she had a child and his father had been killed in the war – all that was true. Her marriage in 1939, however, wasn't and neither was the destruction of her home by a direct hit from a V2 in September '44. She signed the letter *Muriel Matthews (Mrs)* then sealed it in an envelope and posted it before she could change her mind.

The Hamilton's never ever asked about her husband and from the moment they offered her a month's trial they always called her Muriel, never Mrs Matthews. They lived in a four-storey house in Hampstead. Her room was on the third floor. The previous housekeeper had insisted her meals be sent up, but it was so much friendlier to eat with the rest of the staff in the kitchen. The cook adored four-year old James and insisted he eat with them, not with the master's children and their nanny in the nursery upstairs. Also eating in the kitchen were the gardener-handyman, a live-in maid and a girl who came in daily to help with the vegetables and the washing up. As their new housekeeper she listened carefully to their gripes about her predecessor and made sure she never made the same mistakes.

Fourteen years she stayed there: supervising the staff, doing the household accounts, dealing with trades-people, while her son studied hard and passed all his exams at the local school. If she'd had any say in her fate, or a hand in deciding the path she would take in life, this wasn't what she'd have chosen. As it was, however, God had been kind and led her to a safe haven where she could care for the son she adored.

Then in the summer of 1959 James left school and went to university and she knew that her life must change too.

**

As Miss M got up to clear the table, a dizzy turn overcame her. She sat back down and told herself it would pass. She'd just sit here a bit longer.

**

There was no reason for her to remain in service once James had left. She was tired of it anyway: cow-towing to the wealthy. She wanted to do something to benefit deserving people: those to whom life had not been so kind as it had been to her.

It was at the local church that she found out about *The House of Help*. Mr Arlington-Smythe, a very wealthy business man, had bequeathed his Victorian mansion to be used as a home for unmarried mothers and they were looking for a lady of mature years to run it. She was forty-nine at the time. At the interview she had planned to tell the Ladies on the Committee that she would be ideal for the job because she knew exactly how these girls must feel as she had once been in the same position herself. There was no need because she was the only applicant, fortunate really because, looking back, she was sure that if she had told them that she too was an unmarried mother, they would never have offered her the job.

***

Look at the time! She really must clear up, just put the dishes in the sink: she could wash them tomorrow. Halfway between the table and the fridge another wave of dizziness swept over her. The plate, with the rest of the corned beef that she was saving for tomorrow, slipped from her fingers. Her knees buckled and she crumpled onto the stone floor.

CHAPTER 16

"Should've known better"
Richard Marx 1988

Brian wasn't bothered. It was Fiona, his fiancée, who wanted to find out.

'How can you not be curious about your real family?' she said the day they became engaged.

Brian had long ago accepted the fact that he was adopted. "Chosen" was the word his parents had used, conjuring up this vision of a large shop with aisles like a supermarket, his mum and dad walking past rows and rows of babies, picking up one they fancied, turning it over, studying it carefully, then putting it back in case further down the line there was another baby that they liked better. What if one day they decided he wasn't the one they wanted after all and took him back to the shop to swap for one of the others? He tried to be good to make sure they didn't.

When he was five, he'd asked his mum. 'Why was I "Chosen"? Why didn't I grow in your tummy?'

She'd stopped washing the dishes and gripped the edge of the sink. Brian thought she was going to cry. 'Remember we told you. You grew in your other mummy's tummy.'

'But why didn't she keep me? 'Why did she send me to the shop to be "Chosen"?'

'Your mother was just a young girl. She couldn't look after a little baby. Now let's see what we can find for you to do until teatime. How about building a skyscraper with your Lego?'

It was at primary school that the subject came up again.

This time it was Brian who was crying when his mum collected him at the gate.

'Whatever's the matter, sweetheart?'

'It's Kevin. He said I was different because I didn't have a proper mum and dad. I lived with people who couldn't have babies of their own.'

His mum knelt down, held both his hands and looked into his eyes. 'But we love you so much. You're not different. You're special.'

Next day at playtime, Brian told Kevin, 'I'm special and I've got a mum and a dad, not like you who's only got a mum and you don't even have a car.'

Kevin hit him.

Of course, during his adolescence, there'd been times when he couldn't get his own way and he'd used the fact that he was adopted as ammunition to attack his mum and dad:

'I bet my own mother would have let me have one,' he'd said when they refused to buy him a motorbike.

'You're not my real parents. You can't tell me what to do,' he'd said when they caught him smoking.

When they'd grounded him for breaking the 10.30pm curfew, he'd threatened to run away and find his real mum.

He didn't mean it. He'd no intention whatsoever of searching for his real mother. After all she'd given him away, hadn't she? That meant she didn't want him. Why spend time and effort looking for a woman he'd only known for a few weeks, if that? And Brian was a realist. What if he was the result of rape, or a prostitute's child? It wouldn't help him at all to know that, and his mother, who must now be at least in her late thirties or early forties, wouldn't thank him for raking it all up. No point in stirring up the silt at the bottom of the pond, causing mud to swirl through the clear water and ripples to spread out over the smooth surface.

Now, at the age of twenty-one, he liked to think that perhaps he was the result of a rather good time in a secluded circle in the middle of a cornfield, or on the back seat of a Mercedes parked in a lay-by. He also knew that if, when he was six weeks old, he'd had any say in the matter, he himself, would have "Chosen" the parents who chose him. He'd never wanted for anything. He'd followed in his adopted father's footsteps and was now in his final year of a civil engineering degree. He'd met the most wonderful girl and she'd agreed to marry him.

But now she was asking him to find out who his real parents were, something which he knew would upset his mum and dad a great deal.

'No, I can't do it. It's disloyal, after all they've done for me.'

'Don't tell them, then.'

'That's not fair, and anyway I haven't got time for all this until my finals are over.'

'OK, leave it till then.'

Brian shrugged. 'I don't understand why this so important to you.'

'Well, Mummy says that we need to know about your blood relatives in case there's anything that might be passed on to our children.'

'Like what?'

'My sister's friend has a little boy with a cleft lip. She says she can't bear to look at him and he'll need all these operations.'

'So, if you found there was something like that in my family. What then? Would you call off the wedding?'

'No. Of course not. But before the baby's born they can find out if anything's wrong and …'

'And what? What are you suggesting?'

'Well, if any abnormalities show up you can ask for a termination.'

'An abortion. That's horrible. Have you ever thought that I was probably a bit of an inconvenience to my birth mother, but she didn't get rid of me?'

'But you must have been born before abortion was legalised.'

'Oh! great! That makes me feel a whole lot better!' Brian glanced at the diamond solitaire on his fiancée's finger and wondered if perhaps he was making a big mistake.

***

Finals were over by the middle of June. The wedding was arranged for September; they would honeymoon in the Seychelles. On their return they'd move into their new home and Brian would begin working for his father. The firm that up until now had been called *Walters Builders*, would become *Walters & Son*. Three years should be long enough to learn how to run the business, his father had decided, because when he reached sixty-five, he was planning to sign it all over to his son.

Now there was no excuse: Brian had the whole of July and August in which to trace his birth mother. It took ages to fill in the form to apply for his birth certificate and he assumed it would also take months to process. That wasn't the case. Mr Hoskins, a local social worker, wrote back within a week suggesting he ring and arrange an appointment. Brian had used Fiona's address on the form to make certain there was no chance of his mum and dad finding out. So as soon as the letter arrived, Fiona knew about it and insisted that he phone the next day. When he didn't, she did it for him explaining that she was Brian's fiancée, soon to be his wife, and she should also be present, but Mr Hoskins was adamant: Brian was to come on his own.

The office was in a prefabricated building in the grounds of the town hall, a small, pokey room with just enough space for a desk, two chairs and a filing cabinet. Clouds of smoke greeted Brian when he opened the door.

'Have a seat.' Mr Hoskins laid his pipe on the ashtray. 'I believe you want to trace your birth mother.'

'That's right.'

'You're twenty-one. What's made you decide to look for her now?'

'I'm getting married soon. My fiancée thought I should try to find out more about my blood relatives.'

'Ah yes, the young lady I spoke to on the phone. It was her idea then?'

'Yes. Why?'

'Well, it's very important to examine your motives. What do you expect to happen if and when you find your mother?'

'I'm not expecting anything.'

'Do you realize you might not like what you find? Are you prepared for absolutely anything? She may be very different from how you imagine her.'

'I've never seriously considered what she's like. After all I've already got a mother who's been there for me ever since I was six weeks old.'

'How does she feel about this?'

'I haven't told her.'

Mr Hoskins sucked in his lips. 'Might be best to mention it now. If we find your birth mother, your parents are likely to find out then.'

'But it's not as if I'm going to keep in touch with her. I just need to find out about my background, that's all.'

'Well, we'll proceed with obtaining a copy of your original birth certificate, but I'm just not sure you've really thought this through.'

'I have.' Brian put his hand in the inside pocket of his jacket and produced the small, yellowish piece of paper printed in red. 'You'll need this, but it only has my adoptive names on.'

'I know, but that and the date at the bottom will lead us to the original. It'll be on file in St Catherine's House. Leave it with me. I'll contact them.'

'And you'll get them to send me the certificate?'

Mr Hoskins shook his head. 'Oh no, it will come to me.'

'So, I'll have to come and see you again?'

'That's right. I'll let you know when it arrives. In the meantime, I'll also contact the agency that arranged your adoption and get them to send over the files. They may give you all the information you need about your background and you might not need to contact your mother at all.'

'Thank you.' Brian stood up to leave.

Mr Hoskins had already replaced his pipe in his mouth and was reaching for a packet of Swan Vestas before his client closed the door.

Well, he'd done what she had asked so hopefully Fiona would now stop going on about it. The appointment hadn't taken as long as he'd thought, so this wouldn't be a wasted afternoon after all. Brian turned in through a farm gate and came to a halt in what had once been the farmyard. A labourer stopped shovelling and nodded. 'Morning'.

Although he wasn't yet officially on the payroll of *Walters*

Builders, his father had asked him to call in and check that the work was on schedule. Brian, however, had a second reason for coming: one of the luxury modern dwellings fitted into the shell of the old farmhouse and outbuildings was to be his – a wedding present from his parents. The foreman appeared and assured him that the whole project would easily be completed by mid-September and took him on a tour of the converted stable block. It was just as he and Fiona had planned: three bedrooms with exposed beams in the loft, through lounge and dining room on the ground floor. The plumbing was in place for the washing machine and dishwasher in the state-of-the-art kitchen, and for the bidet and double walk-in shower in the luxury bathroom.

Brian walked back to the car past cows grazing in the fields, a small copse and a stream. The only evidence of the city was a few plumes of smoke rising over the hills, way in the distance. When the builders had gone, the only sounds would be birdsong, the lowing of cattle and water meandering down to the lake. What an ideal place to live. What a great place for their children to grow up.

Driving back, his thoughts returned to the social worker and what he had said. He'd seemed quite astute, had realized that it wasn't him but Fiona who was keen to find out about his real parents. It was almost as if he was hinting that it would be best to abandon his search before he'd even started. Well, he'd said it would be several weeks before the birth certificate arrived, perhaps in the excitement of preparing for the wedding Fiona would forget all about it.

When he reached home his mum was baking. Brian made them both a cup of tea, placed hers on the worktop beside her, so she could sip it as she worked, then sat down at the kitchen table. Mr Hoskins had said he should he tell her about the search for his birth mother. He racked his brains for words to cushion the hurt it would cause, but there weren't any.

'You alright, love? Something on your mind?'

Brian looked up at the concern on his mum's face. The wrinkles were beginning to betray her age, but not her hair: only her hairdresser, her husband and son knew that beneath the blonde it was now pure white.

'I'm fine, Mum. Just thinking about the wedding.'

***

'There's a letter from the social worker.'

Drat! Why was it that when you needed something urgently your request got lost under piles of papers on someone's desk, yet when you hoped they'd drag their feet, officials became super-efficient. Now Fiona wouldn't let it go until he'd rung up and made another appointment to see Mr Hoskins.

The same dense fug greeted Brian as he entered the office. The social worker slid the long thin form with the red printing across the desk. 'Your birth certificate.'

Brian scanned the looped handwriting in the boxes. His date of birth. Yes, that was the day he celebrated his birthday. His first name was Brian; how considerate of his adoptive parents to keep the name his birth mother had chosen. He had expected the column headed Name and Surname of Father to be blank; it wasn't. In black ink it said Brian Holmes. Mother's name was Valerie Anne Johnson, so they hadn't been married. It was his mother who had registered the birth. That was useful because it meant her address, 13, Granby Hill, Tooting, South London, appeared in column 7.

So far Mr Hoskins had said very little as he studied

Brian's reaction. 'I haven't received your adoption file yet. Seems there's some problem. The agency closed down in '84. All their records should have gone to the local Social Services department, but they can't locate them.'

'So, what do we do now?'

'We could just wait for the files. They would probably tell you all you need to know about your medical history.'

'Or?'

'We could write to the address on the birth certificate.'

'And if there's no reply?'

'Then it's local electoral roles or telephone directories, sifting through entries with your mother's surname, but that can take years, particularly with a common surname like Johnson. She may have remarried. To find out you'd need to go to St Catherine's House and trawl through their records to see if you can find a subsequent marriage certificate. At the end of all that, you may still not have found her.'

'I think we'll just wait for the file.'

Fiona wasn't too pleased. She was all for them writing to the address on the birth certificate and suggesting a meeting. Brian insisted that if anyone wrote it had to be Mr Hoskins, then if his mother didn't want to know she could just ignore the letter. At least Fiona agreed to that. When Brian put down the phone after calling the social worker he hoped that what he'd been told would turn out to be true: the people now living at 13 Granby Hill might have no knowledge of his mother and the letter would just end up unopened in the dustbin, or returned with the words *Not known at this address* on the envelope.

A week later, Mr Hoskins rang to say the adoption file had arrived and he could fit Brian in that afternoon.

'There doesn't appear to be any mention of inherited conditions,' said the social worker. 'It says here that your mother was sixteen when you were born, your father seventeen. She was still at school and he was a builder's labourer.'

Builder's labourer. Well at least his birth and adoptive family were in the same trade, if at very different levels.

'Your mother's family were C of E. Her father owned a vehicle repair business. Her mother did a lot of charity work, chaired a number of committees.'

'So why did she give me up for adoption?'

'Says here that when the papers were signed, she was in hospital.'

'What was wrong with her?'

Mr Hoskins read further down the page. 'Er…'

Brian held out his hand. 'Can I have a look? After all it is my past life, my family, we're talking about here.'

'But I'm not sure…'

'There's something there you think I shouldn't see, isn't there? Surely you don't think I'm the type to get upset about something that happened more than twenty years ago. I realized long ago there was a chance that my mother was a prostitute, a criminal, a murderess even. She's not, is she? A murderess?'

'Oh! goodness me no.'

'Well, what is it then?'

The social worker pushed the file across the desk.

It was something that Brian hadn't even considered.

The hospital his mother had been in was a mental institution. The report said that although she'd been quite violent and kicked and clawed the nurses when she was first admitted, after a few days she had settled down and become quite docile, a model patient in fact. There had been no previous history of mental illness; it seemed that having a baby so young had precipitated the breakdown.

Mr Hoskins shook his head and murmured, 'It wasn't uncommon, you know, for young girls to react like that when their babies were taken away. Quite understandable, really.'

Brian felt the same. He told Fiona what he had discovered that evening and her mood seemed to change from sunny to cloudy. She asked how long his mother had been an inpatient, and then other questions he found impossible to answer: Had she had any further similar episodes? Did she have to take medication after she was discharged? The only way to find out was to arrange a meeting and ask her, but Fiona, the one who had been all for it, now didn't seem very keen to meet his birth mother. Well, that was fine by Brian; he hadn't wanted to dig up buried secrets in the first place. Now his mum and dad, the people that had been there for him for the last twenty-two years, never need know he'd been digging. Brian could look forward to the wedding without worrying that there would be an uninvited guest, another mother, standing there in the shadows.

***

The bridesmaids were huddled together whispering just inside the church door. Brian, seated alongside the best man in the front pew, could see them staring out into the churchyard, then casting furtive glances in his direction. This was the church where he'd been christened in the marble font. There were the stalls where he'd spent Sunday mornings and evenings in the choir singing the high notes in his clear, unbroken voice. Above them was the intricately-carved pulpit where the vicar had droned on while Brian read copies of the *Beano* and later *Playboy* that the other choristers had smuggled in under their surplices. This was the church where, in two weeks' time, he and Fiona would be married.

The vicar checked his watch once again. 'Well I'm sorry, but since the bride is now half an hour late, we'll have to postpone this rehearsal till another time or…' He smiled. '… just do what comes naturally on the day.'

When Brian and his parents got home, there was a folded piece of paper on the doormat. Inside were the words:

I'm so sorry, Brian. There is no easy way to say this but I have decided that I don't want to get married after all.'

CHAPTER 17

"I don't want to talk about it"
Everything but the Girl 1990

Paula stood at the foot of the stairs and yelled, 'Michelle, you nor up yet? It's half past already!'

No reply, so she made her way upstairs. Michelle should have been showered and dressed by now. What was up with her? Paula knocked on her daughter's bedroom door before pushing it open.

'What are you doing lying in bed? Didn't you hear me shouting?'

Michelle was lying curled up facing the wall. She turned her head towards her mother. 'I'm not going in today, Mam.'

'You alright luv?'

'Just period pains, like.'

'It's not like you to stay home for something like that.'

'Well it is today. I'm taking a sickie, right?'

'There's no need to shout. Will I ring and tell them you're not coming in?'

'No, it's OK. I'll do that later when I get up.'

Paula went back downstairs and began clearing the dishes her son and husband had left on the table. As she loaded them into the dishwasher, she heard footsteps on the landing above and the bathroom door close. She crept into the hall and half way up the stairs to listen. The toilet flushed; there had been no sound of vomiting. Relieved, she turned and went back down, telling herself she was worrying for nothing. Hadn't Michelle just said it was period pains? She couldn't possibly be pregnant.

When her daughter reached sixteen, Paula had suggested that she went on the pill. Michelle had refused, telling her to mind her own business and that she had no intention of sleeping with anyone anyway. Paula had bitten her lip to prevent herself from saying: I wasn't much older than you when I got into trouble.

If only she could talk about the heartache she'd been through so that Michelle could learn from her mother's experience. Not that it would make any difference, of course: how many teenagers took any notice of their parents? At that age they all thought they knew best. So Paula had held onto the secret she'd kept imprisoned in her heart for almost twenty-four years.

***

After her so-called friend had blabbed her mouth off, and the gossip about the girl in the fashion department who'd had a baby had spread round the store, Paula had handed Harrods her notice and caught the train back to Liverpool.

When she got home, she thought perhaps her mother had guessed that she'd run off to Blackpool with Gino because she was pregnant, but Mam never said anything. Her father, when pissed, forgot she'd ever been away and, when sober, was only too glad to have another wage-earner to pay the rent and rates on their high-rise flat. Her three brothers were away at sea most of the time. Ten years later when her mother lay dying in hospital, she'd asked Paula if it was it a boy or a girl? Paula had checked there was no one around to hear and whispered: 'It was a girl, Mam. I called her Gina.'

Richard had been seven and Michelle six when their grandmother died. Their father was Dave, a lad Paula had gone out with at school. At sixteen they'd gone their separate ways: Paula had got a job at John Lewis, Dave worked cash in hand for his father, who called himself a builder.

Paula bumped into Dave down the Pier Head, a couple of months after she came back to Liverpool. She told him she'd been down in London, but it was nothing like it was cracked up to be. While she'd been away, Dave had a bust up with his dad and was now apprenticed to a proper building firm. A year later they were married. Paula, now promoted to cosmetics, continued to work at John Lewis until a few weeks before her son was born.

The early years of their marriage had been hard: Dave struggling to set up his own business, *Bodgit & Scarper*. Paula had said that was a daft name: it meant that the firm had to be legit, there'd be no chance of getting one over on the taxman; they'd always have to do a proper job, and if they got a complaint they'd have to go back and fix it. 'That's right,' Dave said, 'and no one's likely to forget our name either!'

Paula was unpaid bookkeeper and secretary, jobs she fitted in between washing nappies, grilling fish fingers and picking toys up off the floor. Dave went out at six-thirty in the morning and came back after six in the evening, his overalls covered in putty and cement. It had paid off, because eventually the business was making enough money for the building society to grant them a mortgage to buy a detached house on a new estate.

***

Paula sat at the breakfast bar in her fitted kitchen: pine units, eye-level oven, separate hob, Italian tiles on the walls, and thought back to the reunion over three years ago now. She'd told Dave that she was going to meet old friends – that was true enough – to go Christmas shopping – that wasn't. But he was too preoccupied with work, well at the time she thought it was work, to ask why she didn't come back with any presents.

She'd gone to the reunion because it was a chance to let it all out, to talk about Gina to people who knew the great sense of loss she felt, who would listen and wouldn't go shouting their mouth off. But when she got home it had been hard to cram all that stuff back in the box, shut the lid and throw away the key.

Gwyneth seemed to be able to, or so she said during the journey home on the train, but that wasn't right, was it? If it was, she wouldn't have come, would she? But she was adamant: she didn't want to meet her daughter. Eirlys had a new life and if they found each other she'd ask questions – questions that were better left unanswered.

Children had been part of Gwyneth's life for over twenty years but only in term time between the hours of nine and three-thirty, and that was enough. She felt no need to get married or have children of her own, anyway now it was too late. She had, however, hinted that there was a man in her life. Paula got the impression he was already married.

But Paula's sympathy for Gwyneth as the other woman had faded when she discovered that her own husband was having it away with the young receptionist at *Bodgit and Scarper*. She'd seen the girl in the passenger seat of Dave's van, but he'd laughed it off, saying that he was just giving her a lift home. Then a friend saw them leaving a restaurant one night when he said he'd been at a club drinking with his mates until two in the morning.

'What d'you mean?' Paula shouted. 'You honestly telling me that my friend don't know what she saw?'

Dave confessed. He promised it wouldn't happen again. The girl was just twenty and he was flattered by her attention. How could he say no when her fluorescent pink sweater and skin-tight jeans had said, "Look at me. I'm here just for the taking."

Paula had looked at the beer-belly beginning to bulge over his belt and said, 'You silly awld git. She was only after whar's in yer wallet.'

A month later Dave came home with plane tickets and a fortnight's hotel reservation in a small town on the west coast of Italy, a second honeymoon he said. Paula couldn't speak. If she'd been able to, she would have told her husband that the resort he'd chosen was less than twenty miles from where Gino was born and raised, the place he went back to after he left Paula in London, alone and pregnant.

When she looked at the map and saw the name of the Italian village where she'd imagined Gino getting married to someone else, raising children, she felt the same pain in her heart she'd suffered all those years ago. But there was no way she could tell Dave the secret she'd kept for over twenty years. The next day, she said a holiday in Italy would be great. Dave assumed her lack of enthusiasm the night before had been because she was still mad, but now his wife had finally forgiven him.

Away from temptation and the worries of work, Dave was once again hers. But he wasn't going shopping; he gave her a fistful of lira and told her to go and enjoy herself. Paula didn't go searching out designer clothes or expensive handbags; instead she took the local bus to Gino's village.

The bus clattered its way round bends and revved its way up into the hills. It all seemed unreal, like the dreams she'd had in the months after she lost both Gino and Gina. Why had she come? What did she hope to gain? It was quite likely that Gino had moved on, and if he hadn't what then? What would she say if she saw him? He probably wouldn't even remember who she was.

The woman behind the counter in the small *negozio* studied her with undisguised curiosity when Paula haltingly pronounced the street name that was indelibly imprinted on her brain. The shopkeeper smoothed down her apron, came to the doorway and pointed up the hill and flapped her hand to the right.

Half way up Paula turned into the narrow street; her stiletto heels skidded on the cobbles as she tottered down the slope between the four-storey buildings with cast-iron balconies and wooden shutters. She stopped when she reached 21, the house number she'd put on the envelopes of the three letters she'd written after Gina was born. Then she sat down on a low wall in the shade to watch and wait.

Despite the Mediterranean heat, she felt a chill in her bones as in her mind she was once again the teenager waiting in the Mersey mist. Waiting for her fellar, a dark, handsome stranger, to come out of the Italian restaurant where he worked and take her to some secluded spot down the Pier Head.

She tried to recall Gino's face, but the passing of time had blurred his features, only his deep-set, dark eyes and his jet-black hair remained in her memory. A man came out of the door she was watching; there were flecks of grey in his dark hair. Could that be his father? Paula realised that, after twenty-three years, it could be Gino, himself.

This could be the man constantly in her thoughts for more than a year after he left, the swine who had abandoned her and yet she had secretly wept for, so many times. The man banished to her subconscious when she married Dave, only to return at night in her dreams, or when she day-dreamed of how things might have been. What did she feel now? Traces of love peeped out from beneath the layer of desertion and betrayal.

A girl in her late teens or early twenties with the same olive complexion was walking towards the house. The man stopped and they embraced. Was she his daughter? How many other children had Gino had with the childhood sweetheart he came home to marry?

Paula sat there, imprisoned within her memories, until the girl had gone into the house and the man was out of sight. Then common sense took over: the people she'd seen were Italian and they lived in the house that she'd addressed the letters to, all those years ago. That was all. There was no other reason to suppose that man she'd just seen was Gino.

If she was realistic, she knew that it was highly unlikely she'd ever see Gino again … or Gina. Where was her daughter now? In England somewhere she guessed. Did she know she was half Italian? Did she have dark hair that swept, shiny and sleek, down to her waist, like the young girl who had gone in through the door of number 21? Paula remembered the tuft of unruly black hair that wouldn't lie flat no matter how often she brushed it. She knuckled back the tears and walked back up the hill to the bus stop.

Dave couldn't believe it when she arrived back at the hotel without a single package or carrier bag. That night as they lay in bed after making love, Paula looked at her husband's very British features: his pale skin now pink and his brown hair now bleached by the Mediterranean sun. This was the man she'd spent almost half her life with, the man she didn't want to lose. She could never risk telling him about Gino … and Gina. Even if he could accept what had happened years ago, he would never be able to forgive her for deceiving him for all this time. After all it was trust, things like that, that mattered in marriage.

***

When Dave had suggested they go back to Italy this summer, she had shaken her head and they'd booked a fortnight in Barbados instead. Paula slid off the stool, took her mug from the breakfast bar to the sink and poured away the tea she'd allowed to go cold. While she'd been sitting there thinking about the past, there'd been no movement above. She crept up the stairs again, along the landing and peeped into her daughter's bedroom. Michelle was still asleep so she tiptoed away. Downstairs in the lounge she flipped through the address book until she found the number of the hairdressing salon where Michelle worked, then picked up the phone.

'This is Mrs Baker, Michelle's mother.'

'Is she feeling better?'

'Oh, has she phoned in already?'

'She did yesterday.'

'Yesterday. I…' Paula hesitated.

'But said she'd probably be in today.'

'Well, she's asleep just now, so she won't be back before tomorrow.'

Paula replaced the phone, a frown creasing her forehead. The previous day Michelle had gone out at eight-thirty, as usual, and come back just after six. So, where had she been all day?

It was late afternoon before she got an answer. Michelle padded downstairs wrapped in her towelling bathrobe, her

194

hair still frizzed-up from sleep. She flopped down on the sofa next to her mam.

'You look dreadful.'

'I feel dreadful.'

'I phoned work to say you were sick.'

'You shouldn't have done that. I told yer I'd do it.'

'They said you weren't in yesterday either. Where were you?'

'None of your business.'

'It is while you live in our house.' Now she thought about it, Paula didn't remember seeing any packets of tampons lying around in the bathroom for a couple of months. Neither had her daughter asked her to call in the chemist when she went out shopping. 'You're not pregnant, are you?'

'No.'

'So, what's the matter then?'

'Nothin.' Michelle turned away from her mother and stared at the amoeba-like bubbles as they snaked up the lava lamp.

'You can't fool me, Chuck. I know there's somethin' wrong.' Paula picked up a packet of Superkings. 'Here, have a ciggie and tell us about it.'

Michelle put one hand to her mouth and waved the cigarettes away with the other. 'I told you, nothin's the matter.' She got up, walked over to the French windows and looked out at the rain beating down on the patio.

'Wherever it is it can't be that bad.'

Michelle swung round to face her mother. 'If you really must know I had an abortion.'

'What! Without telling me!'

'How could I tell yer? Yer always on about taking the

195

pill, being careful.'

Paula froze. This was a scenario she'd never even considered. She swallowed hard to try and rid herself of the nausea that was rising up into her throat. This was all her fault.

She got up from the sofa and, with unsteady steps, walked over to the window and put her arm round her daughter. 'I'm so sorry.'

Michelle pulled away.

'I was only thinking about you. Didn't want you getting hurt, like.'

'Hurt. Well I'm hurting now, aren't I?' Mascara, not removed from the day before, followed the course of tears down Michelle's cheeks. 'I wish I hadn't done it, Mam.' This time she didn't resist as Paula put her arms round her quivering shoulders.

Paula cried too. She drew her daughter close. They clung together, not speaking, each with their own regrets as outside the rain lashed against the French windows.

Paula knew that now wasn't the time to say no, she shouldn't have done it, that somehow they would have managed: Michelle could have stayed at home to have her baby or if she'd preferred to do it alone, together they could have persuaded Dave to pay the rent on a flat. She couldn't tell her that, now that there wasn't gonna be any baby.

Neither could she tell her daughter why she'd kept harping on and on about contraception, not getting pregnant. If she ever found out that, at her age, her mother had been in exactly the same situation and as a result, somewhere out there, she had a half-sister it would only make Michelle feel even worse.

CHAPTER 18

"A Little time … to think it over"
Beautiful South 1990

'Has anyone in your family ever suffered from heart disease, epilepsy or diabetes?'

Anna finished tying the laces of her Doc Martens and came out from behind the screen. 'I don't know.'

'You don't know?'

She sat down and looked across the desk at the doctor. 'I'm adopted.'

'Oh, I see. And the father. How about his family?'

'I'm not sure.' She hadn't seen Stuart for over a month. Wasn't sure if she'd ever see him again. It wasn't as if they'd decided to have a baby … or decided not to have one for that matter. It just happened.

Anna walked out of the surgery and down the road to the bus stop still trying to take it in. She was twenty-three years old, single and pregnant. She could see her adoptive dad's sneering face, hear his words: "Like mother, like daughter". That's if Mr Harris, as she now thought of him, ever found out. He wouldn't since neither she, nor Brenda, her adoptive mum, had seen him since the day he walked out, five years ago.

Five years in which she'd achieved what? Survived drama school, come away with a diploma and lots of big ideas which came to nothing. The only acting she'd done had been with a touring company who performed in secondary schools: short, controversial pieces on truancy, teenage sex and drugs, designed to promote classroom discussion and hopefully curtail the rise in glue sniffing, pot smoking and unwanted pregnancies. Well it hadn't done much good in her case had it?

The bus pulled up. Anna climbed to the top deck where she lit a cigarette. She couldn't blame Stuart for this; no doubt he'd just assumed she was on the pill, like any sensible girl of her age. She had intended to go to the doctor and get a prescription, but never quite got around to it. Perhaps it was some subconscious thing: she actually wanted a baby. When you have no blood relations the only way to get one is to give birth yourself.

***

When she first found out she was adopted, all Anna could think about was finding out who she really was. Then came the thrill and the apprehension of going to drama school: a whole new beginning: workshops to attend, lines to learn and parties to go to. She'd had no time or inclination to look for her birth mother. But during the touring days when she tired of playing the same show week after week, she'd stare at the rows of faces in the school hall and wonder if her birth mother had any more children? Could her half-sister or half-brother be out there?

When the tour had come to an end, she'd gone back home and been shocked to find that Brenda had a "boyfriend". Her adoptive mother was sixty, for God's sake, and acting like a girl in her twenties … all over a retired plumber.

Anna had been living at home, auditioning for parts she didn't get, for a couple of months when she found the business card of *Forever Families* that Miss M had given her. It had lain hidden and forgotten at the back of her make-up drawer. She'd gone out to a call box to ring the number but it was now an introduction agency and the young girl who answered the phone knew nothing about *Forever Families*. Rather than go straight home Anna sat on a bench in the park and wondered: What did she do now? Go back and see Miss M? But she couldn't afford the train fare, not until she got another job. Anyway, the old lady most likely wasn't there anymore, might even be dead. She'd just have to speak to Brenda. There might be something she knew that would help. Perhaps now that she had a new man in her life she wouldn't get so upset.

As it happened, she never got the chance. The husband Brenda hadn't seen for five years came around pleading with her to take him back, saying she was the one he'd always loved. Anna thought it was far more likely that his mistress had ditched him. Brenda must have thought the same, because she decided she wanted a divorce, let him have the house, took her share in cash and moved in with the plumber. The following week Anna started a job on a supermarket checkout, and moved out. The only alternative accommodation Anna could find at such short notice was a room in a shared house. It was there she'd met Stuart.

***

Anna pressed the bell and clomped her way down the stairs. The bus lurched to a stop at the end of her street: a litter-strewn cul-de-sac with several wheel-less cars propped up on bricks. She stopped outside one of the identical three-storey terraced houses where the front door opened directly onto the pavement. On the one and only occasion Brenda had come to visit she'd said: 'Not the best area to live. Can't you find somewhere better?'

Inside the silence was unsettling: New Kids on the Block, Madonna and Rod Stewart not blaring from under locked doors and competing for attention as they reverberated around the linoleum-floored hall, staircase and landing. The smell of half-eaten Pot Noodle and chip papers was beginning to fade since Anna had emptied the bins and made an effort to wash the kitchen floor. She bent down to pick up the post. There was just one letter for her. She gathered up the rest and balanced them on top of the pile on the hall radiator. The students, including Stuart, had all gone home for the long summer vacation. Some of them wouldn't be coming back: she kept meaning to sort out the mail and forward it on.

In her room she glanced at the letter. It was from the bank, probably a reminder about the overdraft; she propped it up, unopened, on the dressing table, lay down on the mattress and stared at the geometrically-patterned wallpaper that refused to be hidden by the coat of white emulsion that, with Stuart's help, she'd painted over the top. This house with its shared kitchen where grease caked the cooker and dishes piled up in a sink full of murky water was no place to bring up a child.

She kneaded the flat area between her hip bones. There was still time to get rid of it. After all, its conception could quite easily not have happened if they'd had sex just a couple of days sooner, a couple of days later. Anyway, what was abortion but a delayed form of contraception? So how did she go about it? She needed to think; she needed to find out.

There were organisations to help, weren't there? She was sure that she'd seen adverts and unconsciously read questions like: Do you think you might be pregnant? Are you not sure what to do? Do you need someone to talk to? Well now she was, and she did.

Where had she seen these posters? Maybe it was in the

library. Back then it had little relevance to her so she couldn't be sure. She had to do something, not just lie here and worry, so she pulled on her Doc Martens and rummaged around among the clutter until she found the library books which were already three weeks overdue.

As she returned the books, Anna saw the information she needed on the notice-board behind the librarian. Memorizing the number, she went behind the bookshelves to write it down. As she stuffed the pencil and paper back in her pocket, she glanced at the titles on the shelves; one in particular caught her eye. *From Conception to Birth*. Anna walked away then stopped and checked there was no one around. Back in the baby and childcare section, she took the book down from the shelf and thumbed through the pages, stopping at *8 to 12 weeks*. Alongside a crescent-shaped diagram were the words: *At eight weeks the foetus is just over three inches long and the limbs have begun to develop. The arms and legs already have rudimentary fingers and toes.*

Anna placed her hand over her stomach. Inside was the beginning of a human being. For the first time since the doctor had confirmed what, up until then, had only been a slim possibility, Anna realised the enormity of what was happening to her. She replaced the book, her other hand clutching the shelves to stop herself from crumpling into a heap on the floor. Stop being so stupid, she told herself, brushing away the tears with the back of her hand, as she concentrated on putting one foot in front of the other to get out of the library. People she passed on the pavement stared, or hesitated, perhaps wondering if they should stop and ask her what was wrong. Going around and around in Anna's mind was the question: what if her mother had got rid of her?

Up until now she'd never noticed pregnant women; now they were everywhere: in the street, at the cinema, queuing up at her checkout, even working at the supermarket. Anna was asked to cover while a supervisor went on maternity leave.

'It'll be on a higher grade,' the personnel officer said.

More money, thought Anna. She could pay off the overdraft, then start saving up for the baby.

'But if she comes back, then I'm afraid you'll have to return to your original position.'

'You mean she might be coming back?'

'Yes. It's the law. We have to keep her job open so she can return after the baby's born.'

On the way back to her checkout, Anna smiled to herself. She could just imagine his face when in a few months' time she went back to personnel to tell him that she would also need maternity leave. But now at least she could see a way forward; there'd be a job waiting for her to go back to. She didn't need a man's wages to be able to keep her baby. She wouldn't be forced to do what her birth mother had done and give it away.

When she arrived home, there was that illicit smell that had been absent from the house for the last few months. She traced it to Stuart's room; he was inside lying on the mattress, a joint in his hand.

'What are you doing here?'

'Thought you'd be pleased to see me. Term starts next week. Don't tell me you'd forgotten.'

'Why didn't you write over the summer?'

He shrugged. 'Meant to.'

'I'll bet.'

'Well, I had to do some work for the re-sits.'

'Did you pass?'

Stuart nodded.

He looked even more of a mess than she remembered: several days' stubble on his chin, ripped and unwashed jeans. How could she ever have fancied him?

'When I didn't hear from you, I thought you'd failed and wouldn't be back.'

'So, are you glad to see me?' he asked.

Anna had already decided not to contact Stuart to tell him he was going to be a father. If she saw him again, she'd tell him, if she didn't, she wouldn't.

He was staring at her now. 'Is there something wrong?'

'Well not wrong exactly.'

'What then?'

'If you really want to know, I'm pregnant.'

'Christ!' Stuart ran his hands through his shoulder-length, greasy hair. 'You're going to have an abortion, right?'

'Wrong.'

He stared down at her stomach then back up at her face. Leaving his joint smouldering in the ashtray, he got up and put his arms round her. 'We could get married,' he muttered almost inaudibly.

Anna pushed him away and looked into his eyes, saw them pleading, pleading with her to say no. 'You don't mean that.'

'I do. When I get my degree, we'll be fine.'

'What makes you think I won't be fine on my own?'

'When's it due?'

'December.'

Stuart relit his reefer and took a couple of drags before offering it to Anna.

She shook her head.

Avoiding eye contact he said, 'Well, we'll struggle for a few months, but I'm sure my folks will help out.'

'And the baby crying all night will give you yet another excuse if you don't pass your finals.'

'But there'll be a reason for me getting down to some hard graft won't there? To get a job, a house for you and the baby.'

Stuart, always the dreamer, thought Anna. She shook her head. 'It would never work, would it?'

The next person to tell was Brenda. Anna put it off, for fear of how she would react. For all those years she had wished for a baby of her own and now her adopted daughter had become pregnant without even trying.

She had never been to the new house that Brenda shared with the retired plumber. It was on a modern housing estate among a large number of homes all of the same basic design with mix-and-match differences: plain bricks or pebbledash, porches with either pitched or flat roofs, bowed or standard windows, just to make potential purchasers think they were getting something unique.

As she waited for someone to answer the door Anna looked down at the baggy sweater and hoped it concealed her almost five-month bulge, so that she could break the news gently.

It wasn't until she'd been on a conducted tour of the house and heard all about their summer holiday in Ireland that Anna felt able to broach the subject of her visit.

'I've something to tell you.'

'You're getting engaged.' Brenda rose to come over and give Anna a hug.

'No.'

'A boyfriend, then?'

'No. I'm pregnant.'

Brenda sat back down and exchanged glances with the plumber beside her on the sofa. 'But I thought you just said you don't have a boyfriend.'

The plumber reached out for his partner's hand. 'But what about the baby's father. He should take some responsibility.'

'He offered to marry me.'

'Well that's all right then.'

'I'm not going to … marry him.'

'Well, you don't really have much choice, do you?'

Anna clasped her hands together to stop them from shaking. What right did the plumber have to judge her, to tell her what to do? She looked at the woman who had raised her. 'What do you think?'

Brenda looked past Anna and out of the window. 'It's not fair. It's not fair. I tried my best to bring you up properly, to know right from wrong, but in the end it's right what they say: "Bad blood will out".'

Anna stood up. She wasn't going to stay here any longer, listen to this. She had expected her adoptive mum to be upset, but not to blame it all on her birth mother, a woman she knew nothing at all about.

As she walked down the avenue Anna could feel the eyes of the neighbours watching, trying to decide who she was. And who was she? No relation at all to the two people she'd just visited, especially the plumber. He was what? – her adoptive mother's lover. And her, how could she be so horrible, talk about her birth mother like that? How she wished she'd told them that they were hardly in a position to point the finger: They weren't married either.

Stuart cut his hair, started going to lectures and doing

some preparation for tutorials. Anna was adamant, however, there was no way he was moving back into her bed. Sometimes they shared meals but that was all; they still had their own separate rooms. As soon as she found somewhere big enough for herself and the baby, Anna was moving out.

The flat she eventually managed to rent wasn't much better, but at least there were two rooms and she wouldn't be sharing a kitchen; there'd now be some incentive to keep it clean. It wasn't available until November, by which time she'd already be on maternity leave with only a few weeks left before the baby was born.

Stuart insisted on helping with the move. He borrowed his father's car and they made two trips, ferrying the rug, the curtains and the crockery, the Moses basket and the packets of disposable nappies. Anna stood in the centre of the room that served as both kitchen and sitting room, surrounded by plastic bags and boxes. Stuart offered to help her put things away, but Anna shook her head: one thing would lead to another and he'd end up moving in as well.

Before he left, he produced a wad of notes and pushed it into her hand.

'Where d'you get that?'

'It's not mine. It's from my parents.'

'What? You told them!'

'Well, yeah. I hope you don't mind.'

'I thought you wouldn't want your mum and dad to know.'

'Well I do and I'd like to see the baby when it's born and afterwards. Is that OK?'

'Of course it's OK. You seem to forget I've never known my real father. I wouldn't want that for my baby.

And do you realise your parents will be the only real grandparents it will have?'

***

A week before her due date, Anna woke up with an ache low down in her back. Was this the beginning? She didn't know. Had she, herself, been born early? She had no mother to ask. There was no one to tell her what labour was really like, no one who'd been through it themselves. Even the midwife didn't have any children.

By teatime the pain had moved around to the front and she knew this was it. Wait until the contractions are five minutes apart and then go to hospital, it said in the leaflet. But what if that wasn't soon enough? The pain came again. Anna dialed 999.

She arrived at the hospital in plenty of time.

At four in the morning, the midwife said, 'Just rest for a while before the next contraction.' She rubbed Anna's back. 'It shouldn't be much longer.'

Not much longer. She'd arrived at the hospital at six o'clock, ten hours ago. How long had her mother's labour lasted when she was born? Had it hurt as much as this? She too hadn't had a husband beside her, holding her hand, mopping her brow, saying how brave she was.

She had thought of phoning Stuart after calling the ambulance, but in the end decided against it: didn't want him to think that they had a future together. They hadn't. The days of having to get married, to give the baby a name, were long gone. The baby would have her surname. Stuart's name would be there on the birth certificate and her child would get to know its real father, would not be like her and go through life wondering. The next contraction came. Perhaps she should have called Stuart after all: at least she would have been able to scream at him, swear at him.

Anna's baby was born at eight-fifteen in the morning – a girl weighing six pounds three ounces. Before cutting the cord, the midwife laid her on Anna's stomach: the skin to skin contact was made, the mother-baby bond cemented before the blood connection was severed. She looked down at the tightly-closed eyes, the wisps of hair matted to the scalp, the tiny chest fluttering to take in her first breaths and felt this overwhelming need to cherish and protect this new, helpless being. The strength of her feeling surprised her; there was no way she could be parted from her own flesh and blood. How could her own mother have been so heartless as to have given her first-born away?

The next few hours passed on a wave of elation, under a haze of exhaustion.

'Time for a feed, Mum.'

The nurse standing beside her bed had called her Mum. The responsibility was scary. What did she, Anna, know about motherhood? Not until now had the full implication of being a parent really sunk in.

'Let's make you comfortable.' The nurse adjusted the backrest and propped Anna up with pillows, before lifting the baby from the cot at the end of the bed. 'What are you going to call her?'

'Emma.' She took the baby and cradled her close.

The nurse showed her how to support the baby's head with one hand and use the other to lift her breast so her nipple touched the tiny lips. Little Emma responded by opening her mouth, and as the gums latched on Anna winced in pain, not an unpleasant pain, more an initiation. Had she been breast-fed when she was born? It was possible, she supposed, in the six weeks her mother had looked after her. Then she remembered the babies' bottles on the bookshelves in the library at *The House of Help* and she thought, probably not.

That evening at visiting time, Anna asked the nurse to draw the curtains around her bed; the best plan was to hide behind them while all the other mothers on the ward entertained their visitors. Then they wouldn't look over at the empty chair next to her bed, whisper and cast pitying glances in her direction.

'Can I come in?' Brenda was holding the edges of the curtains and peering through a gap.

'After what you said …'

'I didn't mean it. It was just such a shock.'

Anna shrugged.

'I'm sorry.'

Well, Anna thought, at least the plumber wasn't with her. 'OK. How did you know I was here anyway?'

'It was Stuart.' Brenda sat down in the armchair next to her bed. 'He phoned.'

'How did Stuart know?'

'He called round to see you. The couple in the ground floor flat had seen the ambulance. Stuart's waiting outside. They won't let him in until you say it's all right.'

'But they let you in?'

'Well I am your …'

'I only meant that they didn't know who you were, either.'

'Well, at least we still have a surname in common. Oh let's not argue. I came to see you and the baby.'

Anna parted the tightly wrapped shawl with her fingers. 'She's beautiful.'

The rosebud mouth opened to yawn, raising the

eyebrows to furrow the forehead, before emitting a soft little grunt.

'She looks just like you did as a baby.'

'Really. I thought that I was six weeks old when you got me.'

'They showed us a photo of you a few weeks before.'

'I'm sorry.' Anna had noticed the tears collecting in the corner of Brenda's eyes. 'Here, would you like to hold her?'

Brenda scooped up the baby and held her against her chest, one hand under her bottom, the other supporting her head, so the half-open eyes peered over her shoulder. The tiny fingers were curled round into fists and held against her jacket as Brenda swayed back and forward cooing into the baby's ear. 'He seems a nice boy does Stuart.'

Anna shook her head. 'I'm not going to marry him, if that's what you're thinking.'

'It will be hard with a baby on your own. Unless you're going to …'

'Of course I'm not going to … How could you even think that I'd give her away?'

'Ssh! She's asleep now. Shall I put her down?' Brenda moved over to the cot and laid Emma on the pink sheet and covered her with the pink blanket. 'Oh! I almost forgot …' She bent down and took a small package from her bag. '… to give you this. I found it when I was clearing out the house. Dad's selling up, you know, moving to Spain with his latest floozie.'

'I wish you'd stop calling him that. He's not my dad.'

'What shall I call him then?' Brenda handed Anna the package.

'Keith. That's his name, isn't it?' Anna said as she unwrapped the tissue paper. Inside was a pale pink matinee coat.

'You were wearing it when you came to us. I think your mother must have knitted it.'

The wool felt soft as she held it to her cheek. Anna looked down at her baby and said, 'Look Emma, a present from your grandmother.'

A shadow passed across Brenda's face and she bit hard on her lip. 'And there was a letter. Your d … Keith said he couldn't send it on because he didn't know your address.' She handed Anna the envelope. 'Could have posted it to me to give to you, but he wouldn't think of that, would he?'

After they'd said their goodbyes and Brenda was walking down the ward, she called over her shoulder, 'I'll tell the Sister it's OK for Stuart to come in and see you, shall I?'

Anna nodded. As she watched Brenda walk away, she thought about the way she talked about her ex-husband. They'd got married because they wanted to, not because they had to, and look at them now. If she married Stuart what chance did they have?

There he was now, a grin on his face to match the oversize bouquet, no doubt his mother's idea. He dropped the flowers on the bed and bent down to give Anna a quick peck on the cheek. He was wearing a freshly-ironed shirt and seemed most uncomfortable in the hospital environment.

'You haven't looked at your daughter.' Anna inclined her head to the cot at the foot of the bed.

Stuart stood motionless; his mouth slightly open. His brown eyes stared down at the wrinkled face peeping out from the tightly-wrapped pink parcel. 'I can't believe she's mine.'

'Of course she's yours. What are you suggesting?'

'That's not what I meant. I can't believe that I'm a dad. That if it wasn't for me … I mean us … she wouldn't be here.'

'You can hold her, if you like,' said a passing nurse.

'Oh no!' Stuart stepped back.

'She won't break.' The nurse picked up Emma. 'Here now. Remember to support her head,' she said, holding the baby out to him. She must have seen the fear in his eyes because she added, 'Perhaps you'd better sit down first, in that chair next to the bed. Don't worry, you'll soon get used to it.'

As she looked at Emma asleep in Stuart's arms and the mixture of pride and wonder on his face, the possibility that the three of them had a future together crossed Anna's mind. It would be so much easier if there was someone to share the responsibility.

Anna didn't open the letter until visiting time was over and Stuart had left. She glanced at the address and the signature at the bottom of the page. She didn't know anyone of that name who lived in Fulham.

Dear Anna

I am contacting you on behalf of my mother-in-law. She would write to you herself but in March of this year she suffered a minor stroke.

She tells me that you visited her about three years ago at 13 Granby Hill because you were trying to trace your mother. If you are still searching for her, she has some information that may help.

Yours sincerely
Nina Matthews

The letter was dated June 1988. Why had Mr Harris just ignored it, not bothered to forward it on? Almost two years had elapsed since the letter was written. Now it might be too late.

CHAPTER 19

"Coming out of the dark"
Gloria Estefan 1991

Susan moved the photographs from the mantelpiece onto the rosewood table by the bay window then walked across the room to make sure they were in full view when their visitor came into the lounge.

'Wherever you put them,' said her husband. 'She can't fail to see them.'

'It's important for her to know how I've thought about her all these years.'

'I know.' Geoffrey sighed. 'You've told me, over and over again.'

No wonder he was fed up. Susan had talked of nothing else since the letter from Lambeth Social Services had arrived three weeks ago. But how could she even think of anything else when for years she'd longed for this day. The day she would meet her estranged daughter. They'd only spoken briefly on the phone. Chloe, no Anna. The baby she'd given away was now twenty-four and called Anna. She had been to drama school, and was currently working as a supervisor in a supermarket just to tide her over until she got the next part. There were so many, many other questions Susan wanted to ask: about her childhood, her family, how she felt about being adopted, but these were questions it wouldn't be right to ask on the phone.

Anna had asked her if she had married, did she have any other children, if she had a career, but Susan was sure that what she really wanted to know was why she had given her away, who her real father was and what had happened to him. These too were questions that could only be asked when mother and daughter were alone and could only be answered face to face.

Susan looked again at the black and white photograph that Miss M had taken of little Chloe, then the colour print of herself with her baby on her knee taken by Nina on their last day at *The House*. Both photos had now been professionally enhanced and enlarged and mounted in silver frames. She'd had it done for her daughter's eighteenth birthday, but kept them both in her dressing table drawer … until today.

Footsteps crunched outside on the gravel drive. Anna must be early, but no, it was just the postman. Four letters lay on the doormat: one she recognised as a mail order catalogue, a couple of bills and a long brown envelope addressed to her; the hospital logo next to the stamp told her what it was, but there was only five minutes before Anna was due to arrive. There was no way she was going to open it now. She placed it along with the others on the hall stand and studied her reflection in the full-length mirror.

First impressions were so important. She had changed her mind so many times about what to wear: jeans and a sweater to prove she was still young? No, Anna would know that she must be on the wrong side of forty – only just, mind. A dress and jacket? Too formal. In the end she'd settled for a beige linen trouser suit, size 10 and still too big. All those years of dieting to keep her figure trim and now the weight was just dropping off without her even trying.

'Do I look alright, Geoffrey?'

'Of course.'

'I do so want her to like me.' Susan ran both palms

backwards over her blonde waves then, grasping the hair at the nape of the neck with her fingers, gave it a tug.

'Leave it alone. It looks fine.'

'You won't say anything, will you? She mustn't know.'

'If you say so.' Geoffrey put his arm round his wife's shoulders. 'Now are you sure you're alright, this isn't going to be too much for you?'

What would she do without Geoffrey? It would soon be their twenty-first wedding anniversary: for all that time he'd been there for her, put up with her spending sprees, her mood swings, and now this. Susan looked up at her husband: he still had a full head of hair, albeit grey, and that suave aura that had attracted her to a man almost nineteen years her senior.

'I'll be fine. This is something I must do before …' Susan's voice became just a whisper.

'I know.' Geoffrey kissed her cheek.

The bell chimed. Susan took a few seconds to compose herself before opening the front door. For years she had been searching among passers-by, picking out sophisticated young ladies in elegant clothes, and wondering if they were her daughter and now, here she was standing on her doorstep: a girl with long, unkempt hair, no make-up to conceal the grey shadows under her eyes, wearing an ethnic skirt and Doc Martens.

For several seconds neither of them moved. Should they hug each other? Susan held back, frightened in case such a move was rejected. None of the words she had rehearsed for this occasion seemed appropriate.

Geoffrey broke the silence. 'It's Anna isn't it?' He clasped her hand in both of his. 'My wife has been so much looking forward to meeting you. We both have. Now come along into the lounge.'

Susan gestured towards the antique sofa and when Anna sat down, she took a seat opposite on the chaise longue.

'Geoffrey will make us a drink. Would you prefer tea or coffee?'

'Just a glass of water, please.'

Susan watched as Anna took in the inglenook fireplace, the parquet floor, the Turkish rugs, the Ming vases, but her eyes didn't rest on the photographs.

'You have a lovely home.'

'Yes, I've been very lucky. Now tell me about yourself. What's your family like?'

'Well, Brenda, my adoptive mum's OK.'

Anna had used the name mum not for her, Susan, but for someone else. Another layer of guilt, of regret, was laid on the stack that was mounting within her

'But my adoptive father. I don't think he ever liked me.'

'What makes you say that?'

'I think he was jealous. You see they'd been married for years before I came along and when I did, he didn't get all the attention from his wife anymore.'

'You didn't have any brothers and sisters, then?'

Anna shook her head.

Susan recalled Miss M's reassurances that all the babies went to loving families where there were other children to play with. It was a lie. 'So maybe you thought about me when you were a child.'

'No. Until I was eighteen, I never knew I was adopted.'

'What!'

'Brenda didn't tell me until after her husband left.'

'You mean your adoptive father, he left?'

'I think he'd always wanted to leave, but felt he had to

wait until I'd grown up.'

'So, all that time, when I was wondering what you thought about me, you didn't even know I existed.'

'When I found out, I tried to look for you but then other stuff happened. I left home, started drama school.'

The door opened and Geoffrey came in. 'Water for you, Anna.' He placed the tray with a crystal tumbler, a china mug and a plate of chocolate fingers on the table between them. 'And a black coffee. Well, I'll leave you two to catch up on lost time.'

Lost time, thought Susan: precious moments gone forever. Moments her daughter had spent with a substitute mother. She had hoped that the blood ties and the few weeks they'd shared would have created a bond between them, but no. This girl sitting opposite, taking a sip of water was a stranger. Susan lifted the plate and held it out. 'Would you like a biscuit?'

Anna too seemed to be struggling with her emotions. Her hand shook and droplets of water splashed on the French polished surface as she placed the glass on the table. She accepted a biscuit and stared out of the window as she nibbled round the edges. Then she caught sight of the photographs.

'Is that me?'

Susan nodded.

'I wouldn't have known. Only I recognise the pink matinee coat. Brenda gave it to me and said that was what I was wearing when I arrived.'

'Yes, I knitted it.' Susan struggled to hold back the tears. 'That photograph was taken on the day I gave you up for adoption.'

'What was it like … giving me away?'

'I had to. There was nothing else I could do.'

'Did I look at you? Did I cry?'

'It was as if you knew. You couldn't, of course. You were only a few weeks old. But when I handed you over you must have sensed my despair because you started to howl.'

'Did you say anything to me?'

'There weren't any words to express how I felt. I just kissed you and touched your palm and you curled your little hand around my finger.'

'Then what did you do?'

'Locked myself in my room until my father came to fetch me.'

'Your father, my grandfather?'

'Yes. Your grandparents never even saw you. They were ashamed, you see: their unmarried daughter getting pregnant was an embarrassment. They tried to pretend it never happened.'

'Where are they now?'

'He died a few years ago. She's in a nursing home. Funny really. When I needed her, she sent me away for others to look after me. Now I've done the same to her. But at least she doesn't know, doesn't realise where she is or recognise me when I go to see her. But that's enough about me. Why don't you tell me more about yourself? Have you had any more auditions?'

Anna shook her head.

'You're still at the supermarket?' When Anna didn't answer, Susan continued, 'You know I was thinking. Wouldn't it be better for your career if you lived down here in London? We could help find you a nice flat. Geoffrey would be happy to give you work in one of the galleries, in between jobs.'

'There's something I haven't told you. I have a baby.'

'Oh! So, you have a partner?'

'No.'

'Oh, sweetheart.' Susan got up and moved across to sit on the sofa beside Anna and put her arm round her shoulders. 'Why didn't you tell me before? Surely you knew that I, of all people, would understand.'

'Understand what?'

'Being on your own with a baby.'

'But you weren't on your own with a baby, were you? You gave me away.'

'But …'

'I don't know how you could do it. The first time I saw her I knew that I could never give my little Emma away. Whatever happened. Whatever anyone said.'

Susan looked away. 'You must really hate me.'

'All I know is how much I love Emma.'

'You should have brought her with you.'

'She's only three months old. It would have been almost three hours on the train and anyway Brenda said she'd look after her.'

'Does your adoptive mum often look after Emma?'

'Not really. She was angry when I got pregnant. Thought I should have had an abortion, then couldn't understand why I wouldn't marry Stuart.'

'The baby's father.'

'Yes. We did live together for a couple of weeks after Emma was born but it didn't work out. Stuart complained when she cried and he couldn't hear the TV. Then he started staying out all night. In the end I just told him to go.'

'Maybe it's for the best. I often think about what would have happened if Brad hadn't already been married. I'd have been a GI bride and probably spent the rest of my life regretting it.'

'So, my father was American?'

Susan nodded.

'How did you meet?'

'At a party at an American air base. I was just seventeen.'

'Does he know about me?'

'I told him I was pregnant and then I never saw him again.'

'He went back to the States?'

'Yes, before you were born.'

'Would I be able to trace him?'

'Not sure it would be a good idea.'

'But you know where he lived?'

'Well, from his service number my father managed to find his home address, thought he should be made to pay for what he had done. But the solicitor said it was a waste of time. I had no proof he was the father and it would just be his word against mine.' Susan saw the look of dismay on Anna's face. 'I'm sorry. I shouldn't have said that. I didn't mean to upset you.'

'You say he was already married.'

'Yes, he had two young children.'

'So, I have half brothers or sisters?'

'I suppose so.'

'But you, you never had any more children?'

'No, life can be cruel sometimes.' Susan picked up the china mug and drank the cold coffee.

Anna caught sight of the hands on the grandfather clock. 'I'll have to go soon. I'm catching the four o'clock train.'

'Can't you get a later one?'

'I told Brenda I'd pick Emma up before seven.'

'Geoffrey will drive you to the station, but before you go there's something that I must show you.'

Anna followed Susan up the stairs and into the bedroom where their feet sank into the deep-pile cream carpet and their reflections bounced back and forth in the mirrored wardrobe doors. Susan sat on the bed and patted the satin duvet to indicate Anna should join her. Then she opened a drawer in the kidney-shaped dressing table and took out a small box; inside, nestled in tissue-paper, lay a pair of pink bootees and a lock of hair.

Susan stood in the drive and waved until the car was out of sight then walked back inside and went straight into the lounge where she opened the cocktail cabinet and poured herself a large G & T. The meeting she'd longed for all these years had been a disaster. She replayed the scene in her mind, went over the dialogue. Everything she'd said seemed wrong. What words should she have used? Was there any way she could have made her daughter understand? When she'd asked if they could meet again, if she could see her granddaughter, Anna had replied: 'Maybe, but not yet. I need time to think.' But that was the problem: Susan had so little time.

CHAPTER 20

"Don't let the sun go down on me"
Elton John 1992

Valerie watched as the six dark-suited men, each with a hand raised to balance the coffin on their shoulder, moved one foot then the other in unison down the aisle. How strange: the one on the left at the front was dark-skinned. Well, maybe there were no male relations to carry her body: the pallbearers were just funeral extras hired in by the hour. After lowering the coffin onto the stand in front of the altar they straightened up and receded into the congregation. The middle-aged man who had been at the right front corner slid into the front pew alongside a woman with shiny black hair pinned up in a chignon.

Ever since they'd entered the church, Valerie and Paula had been trying to decide who she was. Why was she sitting there at the front? Who were the children and the young man alongside her? The woman had turned briefly as the funeral procession entered the church and Valerie had thought her face was vaguely familiar.

The minister raised his hands to indicate everyone should be seated, then clasped the sides of the lectern and gazed around the congregation. 'We are gathered here today to remember the life of Muriel Matthews …'

If Valerie hadn't seen the announcement in the *Evening Standard,* she would never have known that Miss M had died. "*… passed away peacefully in her sleep aged eighty-two,*" it said. The funeral was to be held in Fulham. "*Anyone who remembers her from 13 Granby Hill most welcome*".

Should she go? In the end Valerie rang Susan but there was no reply from her London number so she'd tried Paula in Liverpool who'd said she would come down and they could go together. No one knew how to get in touch with Gwyneth.

'We shall begin by singing hymn number 365, *Praise my soul, the King of Heaven.*'

As they stood up, Paula whispered, 'Well I never expected such a lorra people to be here.'

Valerie couldn't help thinking how Miss M, who had led her girls in their feeble attempts at singing in the tiny chapel at *The House*, would be heartened to hear hymns sung as they should be. A voice now and again rose above the rest – slightly off key, the words not pronounced quite correctly. It triggered a response in the recesses of Valerie's brain: Nina. Well, she and Paula were here so why shouldn't Nina be here too.

'Amen.' The minister nodded to the man in the front pew. 'Muriel's son, James, would now like to say a few words.'

Paula nudged Valerie, raised her eyebrows and mouthed the word 'Son'.

Valerie raised her shoulders, pursed her lips and made a slight movement of her head from side to side. The pallbearer sitting alongside the dark-haired woman in the front pew got up to take his place behind the lectern. As he surveyed the mourners, she noticed the dimple in his chin, just like Miss M's. Why had Miss … Yes, *Miss* M never told them she had a son?

He cleared his throat then began. 'I never expected so many of you to be here today, but then I remembered how my mother touched the lives of so many people. She cared for others but was a very private person and hardly spoke about her own life. A life that wasn't easy. My father was killed in the war and she brought me up on her own. Most of the money she earned as a housekeeper was spent on making sure I didn't go without. Then when I went to university, she ran a home for unmarried mothers and I know there is at least one girl that she helped during those years here today …' He paused and smiled at the dark-haired woman in the front pew. '… and at least three of the babies who were born at *The House of Help*.'

***

'Nina and Miss M's son.' Paula said as they walked to the car. 'Would yer believe it?'

'Didn't recognise her at first sitting there in the front pew, so different from the girl in bare feet and jeans.'

'Took her baby everywhere with her. Remember? A boy wasn't it. What did she call him?'

'She didn't.' Valerie rummaged in her bag for the car keys. 'Said in Greece they don't give children names till the christening.'

'Well her baby must be that fellar sat next to her in church.'

'Yes, he's one of the babies from *The House*, but Miss M's son said there were three. What about the other two?' Valerie opened the car door, got in and leaned across the front seats to release the door handle.

Paula eased herself into the passenger seat. 'Must have been hundreds born at *The House*. How long did he say Miss M was there?'

'Nearly twenty-five years.'

'Well one thing's for sure, my Gina can't be here. She wouldn't know about Miss M.'

'She could have found out where she was born, come looking.'

'You're jokin'. If Gina turned up, I don't know whar I'd do. I couldn't tell Dave or our Michelle. They'd never forgive me.'

Valerie stared out of the windscreen. 'Little Brian found me.'

'That's great. You must be really made up.'

'I never met him.'

'How's that?'

'I got a letter from Social Services saying he was trying to trace me. I wrote back, but never got a reply.'

'That's dead mean,' said Paula.

'I thought perhaps he'd had an accident or something, even worried that he was dead. Brian could see how upset I was so he said we should go and see the social worker. Mr Hoskins his name was. He said he'd forwarded my letter.'

'So why didn't Brian write back?'

'Mr Hoskins said it was probably because of the wedding, then the honeymoon, then moving into a new house. When he'd settled down, he'd be in touch … but it's been more than three years now.'

'You must be gutted.'

'I was, but then I decided I'd spent too much of my time wishing for something that wasn't to be, so I decided to get on with my life.'

As the hearse drove past, Valerie turned the key in the ignition then joined the end of the long funeral cortège. On the slow journey to the cemetery Valerie told Paula how she had got a place at university, gained a sociology degree and was now a children's social worker.

On one side of the grave stood James, Miss M's son.

Beside him was Nina with her arm around the youngest girl; next to her was another girl, slightly older, then a boy in his teens and finally a young man.

Paula nudged Valerie and nodded towards the young man. 'That must be Nina's baby.'

When the minister finished the prayers, the family stepped forward in turn and threw a handful of earth on top of the coffin.

Valerie stared down at the soil sprinkled over the brass plate, *Muriel Matthews 1910 – 1992*, and tried to visualise the old lady inside, her one ally all those years ago. If only Miss M hadn't been ill, gone away to recover, leaving Nurse Harding in charge. If she had been there, Miss M would never have let them take little Brian.

People were beginning to drift off, making their way back to the cars.

'You do not remember me?'

Paula and Valerie spun round. 'Of course we do, Nina.'

'We didn't recognise you at first, sitting there in the front pew. Can't believe you are married to Miss M's son. We didn't even know she had a son.'

'You never see the picture of the boy … in her office?'

'On the mantelpiece, short trousers, Fair Isle pullover,' said Valerie. 'I thought he was her nephew or something.'

'Miss M, she tells only the girls who keep their babies.'

'So how come you met him?' asked Paula.

'When Darius goes to school, Miss M she says I should get better job. She knows this day school for disabled children where they need carers. She doesn't tell me that James is a teacher there.'

'So, you got married and have children?' Paula said.

'Yes, altogether with Darius we have four. And you, you

are married also?'

'Yes, and we have children, but not our babies that were born at *The House*. They were taken away for adoption.'

'That is so sad. In Greece it would not happen … and your friend?'

'You mean Gwyneth?' asked Valerie.

'What she is doing now?'

'Went back to Wales, was working as a teacher when we met up a few years ago. We didn't think she'd come to the reunion, but she did.'

'She is married also?'

Paula shook her head. 'But when we travelled home on the train together, she did talk about this fellar. His name was Ger… Oh some Welsh name, like. I think maybe he was already married.'

'Why?'

'Just the way she said marriage wasn't for her. Anyway, it was too late for her to have children so what was the point.'

'Have you heard from her since?'

'About a year ago I got a postcard from Buenos Aires. Said she'd packed in her job and was travelling the world. Didn't sound like she was on her own.'

'Susan came to the reunion too,' said Valerie. 'We tried to phone to tell her about Miss M, see if she wanted to come to the funeral, but there was no reply.'

'Oh.' Nina put her hand to her mouth. 'You did not know? Susan, she died.'

'What?'

'Last year, but her daughter is here.'

'Her baby, Chloe?'

'Yes, but now she is Anna. You come back to the house

and you will meet her.'

'Your husband said there are three babies born at *The House* here today. One is your son, Darius, the other is Susan's daughter, so who is the third?'

'Oh! that is Le-Roy. He and James they carry the coffin.'

'Le-Roy?' Valerie looked at Paula then back at Nina. 'You mean Christine's baby? Christine who cooked Christmas dinner?'

***

James and Nina lived in a terraced house with a thin strip of garden between the bay window and the front wall, so typical of homes built in London at the turn of the century.

James was greeting their guests at the front door.

'Nina's in the back,' he called out.

Paula and Valerie squeezed their way between people in the narrow hallway; to their left were two rooms, also crowded. They passed the foot of the stairs and followed the passage into the breakfast room where Nina was urging everyone to help themselves to the sausage rolls and vol-au-vents, *dolmades* and *klefticos* from the buffet.

Nina saw them hesitate in the doorway and waved. 'You must come to meet Darius?' She turned to the young man standing beside her. 'Here are my friends. I know them from before you were born.'

Darius was a head taller than his mother but had the same dark hair and olive skin.

He smiled. 'Thank you for coming to my grandmother's funeral.'

A frown crossed Paula's face, then she smiled and clasped the hand he held out. 'Of course, when Nina married her son Miss M became your grandmother.'

Valerie shook his hand too, but just couldn't bring

herself to say anything. Inside she was thinking: how could Nina who had no-one when she left *The House* be able to keep her baby, be there for him while he grew up, watch over him for the last twenty-five years, while she, Valerie, had to give her baby away. It didn't make sense; her baby's father had stood by her, but they'd still taken little Brian away.

'Are you alright, Valerie? Come sit down.' Nina led the way to a chair. 'Darius, you get some water.'

'I'm OK. Please don't make a fuss.' Valerie caught Paula's eye. 'I think perhaps we should be going soon.'

'Not yet,' said Paula. 'Not before we've met Chloe … I mean Anna.'

Valerie hadn't noticed Anna at the church or in the cemetery, but when Nina pointed her out, in the kitchen helping to prepare more sandwiches, it was quite obvious who she was: the fair hair, the blue eyes.

'Valerie and I knew your birth mother. We're so sorry to hear that she died.'

'I didn't know she was so ill when I first met her.' Anna bit her lower lip. 'But she already knew she had ovarian cancer.'

'She would be so pleased to find you,' said Valerie.

'She was.' Anna looked away. 'But I was rather hard on her, I'm afraid.'

'It must have been difficult,' said Paula. 'For both of you after all this time.'

Anna wound a tendril of hair round her index finger, just as Valerie remembered Susan used to do when she was anxious. 'I'd just given birth myself, you see, couldn't understand how any mother could give her baby away. It was months before I went back and by then she was much worse.'

'It's not your fault,' said Paula. 'A lorra things have changed. It's hard for young girls like you to understand whar it was like for us unmarried mothers back then.'

'I was with her when she died though and do you know what? She asked if I forgave her and she called me Chloe.'

Your baby's not with you today?' said Valerie.

'She's with her grandad.'

'Her grandad? Oh, you mean your husband's father?'

'No, I'm not married. Emma's with Geoffrey, Susan's husband. I know he's not her real grandad, but he's done more for me than my adoptive father or my biological father ever did.'

'Yeah, Susan's GI walked out on her too … just like my Gino.'

'Before she died, she told me about Brad, where he lived. Miss M warned me not to try and trace him, but I didn't listen.'

'Did you find him?'

Anna told them how she'd written to her birth father. After six months she still hadn't heard, so she phoned. A woman answered. She said yes, she'd seen the letter. It wasn't that she didn't know about all her husband's affairs, but finding out that he'd had a child by another woman, a schoolgirl, had given her the courage to confront him and tell him to leave.'

'Did she tell you where he'd gone?'

'Said she didn't know, didn't care.'

***

It was almost five when they left. Paula was staying overnight with Valerie and catching the train back to Liverpool the following day. As Valerie drove them back to her house, Paula kept on about how things had turned out. Susan and Christine both dying so young. Christine's baby, Le-Roy looking after Miss M, finding her after her stroke, still going to see her after she'd moved in with her son, carrying her coffin. She still couldn't believe that Miss M had a son and that he'd married Nina! And at the funeral Susan's baby, Anna, helping Nina's daughters to wash the dishes. Miss M would have been made up if she'd seen them.

Apart from the occasional "Umm", Valerie said very little. In her mind she was replaying Anna's words. How she'd felt when she first met her birth mother: "Somehow it wasn't at all as I'd expected", Anna had said. "Hard to know what to say. I thought there would be something there, some instant recognition, but there was nothing. I think I wasn't the sophisticated, well-groomed woman she'd imagined. She didn't say so but I could tell … and all I could think of was if I could manage to keep my baby, why couldn't she."

And Anna hadn't been sure that she wanted to see Susan again, hadn't gone back, not until her mother was dying. Then it was too late and now all that Anna was left with was guilt. Perhaps it would have been better if they hadn't tried to find each other, if their paths had never crossed.

Maybe Paula was right in wanting only to be able to watch her daughter from a distance, to peep out from behind a magic curtain from time to time, just to see how she was, to know she was alright, enveloped within her new life – that would be enough. Or Gwyneth, even, wanting her daughter's new life to be her only life, with no mystery, no Pandora's box to open.

All these years and Valerie had lived in hope she'd find

little Brian, couldn't understand why he'd stopped looking for her, but perhaps it was for the best: her own need to see him was just selfish. She'd always assumed he'd be so pleased to find her, had imagined an emotional scene of hugs and tears, but the chances were that the blood bond had been broken years ago. Anna had made her realise that a reunion that didn't work might be even worse than no reunion at all.

'Valerie, whar's up?' Paula had stopped talking and was staring at her. 'You OK?'

'Sorry, what were you saying … about your daughter … was it?'

'Yeah, Michelle. I haven't told anyone about this, but she had an abortion. 'It were my fault.' Paula hesitated and took a deep breath before continuing. 'She said she couldn't tell me, her mother, about the baby 'cos I'd warned her so many times not to get pregnant … but I'd only kept going on and on about it 'cos I didn't want what happened to me to happen to her.'

CHAPTER 21

"Secret"
Madonna 1994

Brian knelt down on the landing in front of the cardboard box he'd just brought down from the attic. His fingers disturbed a layer of black, gritty dust as he picked at the parcel tape, and opened the top flaps to reveal his files from university days. He pulled them out in turn and flicked through the pages of scrawled writing, recalling the hard slog of trying to remember all the technical detail, much of which he had never used in his professional life. Should he keep them or just throw them away?

Inside one of his old textbooks was the letter. He sat back on his heels and took the single sheet from the envelope. The handwriting was small and neat, each letter perfectly formed, each word carefully considered.

5th October 1988
My Dearest Brian,

For the last twenty-one years, not a day has gone past without me thinking of you. I was so pleased when Mr Hoskins contacted me to say that you were trying to find your birth parents.

Please understand it was never my idea that you should be adopted. They said at sixteen I was too young to look after a baby. When I came home from my first day back at school, you were gone. I cried and cried so they sent me away. I never saw you again.

You must have been almost two when your father, Brian, and I got married. We tried so hard to find you, so you could come back to live with us and your new sister, but they said it was too late. You had a new family. I hope they have been good to you.

There is so much more I want to tell you and so much I want to know about you and your life.

I will wait to hear from you and I hope we can meet very soon.

Love

Valerie (Your mother until they took you away at just six weeks old.)

PS Here is a photograph of you with me, your father and your grandparents (Brian's Mum and Dad) and your uncles. It was taken on Christmas Day when you were four weeks old.

Brian took out his handkerchief and blew his nose hard. The first time he'd seen this letter he'd also struggled to control his emotions. It had been on the day of the wedding … the wedding that never happened. Back then he'd thought if only … If only he hadn't let Fiona persuade him to start looking for his birth mother everything would be OK: he'd be putting on his grey morning suit, riding to the church in the white limousine, standing in front of the vicar waiting for his stunning bride to walk down the aisle to join him. During their engagement he'd had a few doubts about whether he was doing the right thing, but everyone had pre-wedding wobbles didn't they? When she'd called it off, Brian could only think of how much he wanted to get married, how much he wanted Fiona.

The letter had lain between the pages of this well-thumbed tome from his university days, in the box along with the other possessions he hadn't needed in Singapore. He had moved over there six months after Fiona had ditched him, to start the new job he'd accepted in an effort to forget all about her.

Now six years on, his vision was no longer distorted by

passion and infatuation and he couldn't remember the last time he'd thought about Fiona, the woman who'd left him because she thought their children would be tainted, would inherit the mental flaws which led to his birth mother being detained in a mental institution.

His mum had been right about Fiona, not that she'd ever said anything. It was just that look that flitted across her face, when his fiancée went on about designer labels or her well-connected family. The same fixed smile he remembered from his teenage years when his mother doubted his cover story for the tentative experiments in the world of alcohol and ecstasy.

Brian's thoughts returned to the present and he re-read the letter. This time he saw the situation in quite a different light: not something that had ruined his life, but something that had saved him from a disastrous marriage. His birth mother, Valerie, no longer appeared as an inadequate person to be pitied, but a victim, condemned by a society that concealed or denied anything that it felt to be shameful or unseemly. Why, oh why, had he been so preoccupied with his own problems that he hadn't seen it this way before? Valerie said she had thought about him every day, searched for him and been so pleased to hear he was looking for her. How must she have felt when she never received a reply to her letter? Her hopes of finding her lost son raised and then shattered. He had to find her. He had to find his birth mother.

'What have you got there?'

Brian hadn't heard Mei Lien come up the stairs. She stood beside him, one hand rubbing the small of her back. He had told her to take it easy; it was only a few weeks until their baby was due. She had insisted on coming with him to help sort out the boxes of toys, school reports, football programmes and university stuff that his parents had stored in their attic for years.

Mei Lien was so different from Fiona: her hair wasn't blonde, but dark, almost black, her skin wasn't pale like Fiona's but a rich coffee colour. Mei Lien was Eurasian, the descendant of a loving but uncommitted relationship between her grandfather, a married planter and her grandmother, one of his tea-estate workers. Her hair was drawn back and held in a bun, often adorned with a flower, accentuating her perfectly oval face.

His wife's serene expression broke into a smile and Brian still couldn't believe how lucky he was. They'd met while Brian was living in Singapore and moved back to England together so that Brian could take over the family business when his father retired. It was a year later, just two days before his parents' fortieth wedding anniversary that his mother had died quite unexpectedly from an aortic aneurism.

His father had been inconsolable for the first year, until a friend had persuaded him to take up golf. Then to Brian's amazement he'd met someone else, a divorcee who belonged to the same club. They were now both selling up and buying a house together.

The letter was still in Brian's hand. Its contents wouldn't come as a total surprise to Mei Lien. He'd told her from the start that he was adopted, but would she understand when he explained that it was society who had ostracized his birth mother, forced her to give up her baby, then, when she protested, hidden her away, and labelled her as insane?

'We need to talk.' He led the way downstairs then put his arm round her shoulders as they walked down the hall to the kitchen. 'Mei Lien, you remember I once told you I was adopted.'

'Yes, but you said you didn't want to talk about it.'

'I know, but things are different now. I'd like you to read this.' Brian pulled out a chair for his pregnant wife to sit down at the kitchen table and handed her the letter.

As he filled the kettle to make coffee, a cold fear crept over him. What if Mei Lien reacted the same way as Fiona?

When she looked up there were tears in her eyes. 'Oh, Brian. How sad. Did you write back to her?'

Brian shook his head. 'The letter came on the day Fiona and I were supposed to get married.'

'But you didn't get married. She called it off, but you never told me why.'

'Fiona found out that after I was born my birth mother spent six months in a psychiatric hospital.' Brian looked down at Mei Lien's stomach and wondered if he'd already said too much.

'Well that's hardly surprising, is it? Imagine, if in a month's time, someone takes our baby away. How do you think I'd react?'

'So, you don't mind?'

'Of course not. What I can't understand is why, after Fiona left, you didn't get in touch with … what shall I call her? Valerie, I think, that will be easier. Why didn't you write back to her?'

'Well I never wanted to search for my birth mother in the first place. It was all Fiona's idea, and there was Mum and Dad. I didn't want to hurt them.'

'But now. Now there's nothing stopping you.' Mei Lien stroked her stomach. 'And there not much time, is there, if we're going to find Valerie before her grandson is born?

That is, if you want to.'

Brian put his arms round Mei Lien and drew her close. 'Yes, I do want to. Together we must find her.'

ABOUT THE AUTHOR

Rosemary Brierley's background is in the NHS and as an associate lecturer with the Open University.

Since her retirement she has been awarded an MA in Writing (with Distinction) from Nottingham Trent University and has been editor of the charity magazine, Tidings. She has had articles and short fiction published in journals, anthologies and magazines.

Her first book, *A Bletchley Park Wren Overseas,* a biography, based on the diary her aunt, Flora Crossley, kept during World War II, was published in 2018.

A House of Help is her first novel inspired by the three months she spent in a home for unmarried mothers in the 1960s.

Rosemary does not participate in social media, but would be pleased to hear from her readers:

rosemarybrierley.writer@gmail.com

www.rosemarybrierley.weebly.com

THE HOUSE OF HELP

Printed in Great Britain
by Amazon